Perennials

Bryce Gibson

Interior Layout & Design ©2013 - BookDesignTemplates.com

Cover Design by Humblenations.com

Perennials/Bryce Gibson. -- 1st ed.
ISBN ISBN-13: 978-1533508188
ISBN-10: 1533508186

For every plant person

Perennial (adj.) – lasting for an indefinitely long time; enduring

–Dictionary.com

1.

the first murder...

ON THE LAST day of her life, Mary Gold left work early.

It was only a little after four-thirty in the afternoon, and she wasn't supposed to leave 'til five. A lot of people wondered if things would've turned out differently if she'd simply followed the rules. Would she have made it home before the killer and successfully locked the door behind herself? Or would she have pulled into the driveway just as he was slipping through the front door, spotted him, and called the police? People realized that there was nothing that Mary could have done to prevent her untimely death. That's the thing about serial killers—they target, stalk, and plan the attack.

Mary slipped the paperwork that she had been working on into a fat, overstuffed, manila folder and placed the entire thing in her filing cabinet. She quietly locked the drawer and took a quick look around her office just to make sure that no one was looking. The coast was clear. She grabbed her purse, flung it over her shoulder, and walked right out of her office, flipping the light switch as she went past.

The roads were pleasantly empty. It felt exuberant to sneak past the five o'clock rush hour traffic. Even though she worked in a small town, the traffic could still be a headache. She needed to pick up a few things on the way home—dinner, dessert, maybe a bottle of wine or two. She wanted the night to be perfect.

After the next intersection, she pulled her car into The Orchard. It was a local, high-end restaurant that served locally grown food, homemade wine, and craft beer. The parking lot was nearly empty, but she knew that she was only narrowly missing the flood of people that would soon be there for dinner.

Trees were painted along the exterior cinderblock wall. The red front door was located within a garden trellis that had green vines growing over it and clear string lights draped all along it.

"Hey," said the girl behind the hostess stand at the front. Her hair was pulled back in a ponytail. Her lips were painted a bright red. She was obviously a college student.

"I'm picking up a to-go order," Mary told the girl.

"Name?"

"Mary Gold."

The girl smiled. Her white teeth looked even whiter against the red lips. Mary was surprised to see that there was not a single smudge of lipstick on them. "Like the flower?"

"Like the flower," Mary said, unenthusiastically.

People often reacted this way upon learning her name. For those that recognized the cute play on words, it usually brought a smile to their face. Mary had heard it so many times that she no longer found it cute. She had long ago lost the ability to see any magic in her name. Sometimes she wondered what it would be like to see it from their perspective; to discover someone had been named after a flower. Would she then be able to see the enchantment?

When Mary got home, she placed the bag of takeout on the kitchen table. She walked across the hardwood floor and placed the bottles of wine in the fridge. She reached to the top of the refrigerator and picked up a clear glass jar that had a yellow candle inside. She lit the wick.

When she turned around, she noticed something on the floor. At first, it was the color that caught her attention. The bright yellow stood out brilliantly against the polished wood slats. She placed the candle on the kitchen island. When she bent over to pick up the flower, wondering where it had come from, she noticed that there were more of them. In fact, there was a trail of them that led through the hallway toward the bedroom.

She twirled the flower around in her fingertips by its stem. It was a marigold. She had recognized it immediately.

How romantic, she thought sarcastically.

Even though he wasn't supposed to be there for another hour, Ben must've arrived early, she reasoned.

It wasn't the first time that someone had given her marigolds. Over the years, she had received them in vases on birthdays and Valentine deliveries at the office. And each time, the man had surely thought how clever he must have been, that he was the first to ever come up with the idea of giving a woman by the name of Mary Gold marigolds.

Today was different though. It could've been that she was already so excited about the evening that she let herself fall under the spell.

She followed the trail of yellow flowers around the door and into the bedroom, careful not to step on any of them. She expected to see Ben there. Or at least several lit candles and a bottle of wine, but all that she saw was more flowers. The bed was covered in them.

Still holding the single flower between her fingertips, she slowly turned around, taking in her surroundings, when she saw movement out of the corner of her eye. She had seen someone walk past the doorway. It had been quick, only a blur of movement and dark clothing.

She coyly began walking back out of the room, holding the flower to her nose. "Playing games, are we? We've got some time before dinner," she said, alluding to something more.

She was standing in the hallway. "Benny," she said. "Come out, come out wherever you are," she playfully called.

The gloved hand grabbed her so quickly that it took her a moment to register what was going on. The grip was forceful and caused her to flinch and jerk away. She swung her arm and managed to break free from the grasp. She turned and ran back toward the bedroom. Her feet slipped on the flowers that were scattered across the floor. Managing to make it across the threshold before her attacker, she slammed the door and locked it. Her heart was pounding behind her ribcage. Her eyes shot around the room. Despite the fact that she was looking for an escape or a weapon to fight back, all she could see was yellow.

The window! She charged across the room and jerked the blinds up. Behind her, the door was rattling. Her hand reached for the latch at the top of the window, and as soon as she had it undone, she was pushing up on the glass. The old counter weights rattled within the window frame.

It was only a moment between hearing the door bang open behind her and feeling the hand grab onto the back of her dress. She screamed while reaching her hands through the window but was pulled back forcefully and thrown onto the bed. In a strange and uncontrollable assault on her senses, the scariest moment of her life was filled with the intoxicating, pungent smell of the flower blooms.

The attacker crawled on top of her, pinning her down. She reached her hand up and fought.

Then she saw the sharp object that was raised high above the maniac's head, ready to come down into her chest. She tried to scream, but the attacker's other hand was covering her mouth. She could taste the leather of the glove as she was impaled with metal.

2.

MY NAME IS Dusty Miller. Before my parents named me they had no idea of the plant that shared the same label that they were about to give their only son. To this day, both of them claim to have never heard of it before then. Back in those days, before me, Momma and Daddy had been young and carefree. Why would they care about such a thing as the name of a plant? I'm sure they had more important things to worry about anyway like what to have for supper, which movie to rent that night, or how to pay for the married life that they had suddenly fallen into.

Sure, they had seen dusty miller plants before, at greenhouses and within the flower beds and planters of other people's yards and porches, but they hadn't known what it was called. Once again, they simply didn't care.

It has been said, I don't know how many times before, that my daddy just liked the name *Dusty*. It was a name that he thought was masculine and rugged. He thought that it held a sense of mystery. And he just so happened to be a Miller, so when the first and surname were placed together, that is what they got.

Dusty Miller.

The plant comes from the family Senecio Cineraria. It prefers full sun, is drought tolerant, and is resistant to insects and disease. I know firsthand that the plant is hardy, even surviving cold winters in most southern areas of the United States. The textured foliage is pretty. In fact, it is the foliage that is the plant's shining star quality. The foliage is a whitish silvery gray. It reminds me of a plant that has just gotten a light dusting of the season's first snow.

Okay, let me stop here and confess. I know that I'm being a tad dramatic. I'll admit that *a light dusting of the season's first snow* is a bit over the top, but it's descriptive and sounds good in the context of what I'm writing. So, if you could please forget the fact that where I live in South Carolina sometimes goes *years* without a single snowflake, much less what a weatherman would call a *light dusting*, and allow me to describe it how I see fit.

So yeah, it reminds me of a plant that has just gotten a light dusting of the season's first snow. I don't remember the first time I was told about my namesake plant or the first time that I saw one in person. It must've been when I was a kid. I mean a *kid* kid, not the seventeen-year-old one that I was when all of this took place. Most of what I know about the plant I learned from my girlfriend, Nan, and her mom, Rose.

I know that it is often used in the borders of both formal and cottage style gardens. I learned that little tidbit from one of Roses' gardening magazines. The plant is sometimes grown in pots. It is an ornamental plant, not really serving much of a purpose but to be pretty, and *to dress up an otherwise drab setting*, as I heard an old lady describe it one time. It does bloom. Yellow. Most people never see the blossoms though. They prefer to pinch the buds off to promote new growth of the foliage. The plants are rarely even allowed to last that long anyway. Dusty miller is often planted as a place holder, if you will, until it is time for something better.

Since thinking so much about the plant, I've often wondered if that is how people see me. It sure is how I feel, like I'm something pretty to pass the time. Okay, I know calling myself pretty is conceited and all, but I do, I hear it all the time and not from just Momma and Daddy, or Gran. My last girlfriend, before Nan, Moira Everson, even told me when she broke up with me that I was easy on the eyes, but, as she smacked on her chewing gum, later added very candidly, *you're also kind of dull and boring.* Not much later she was dating Bartley Vance.

I have blue eyes, fair skin, and dark hair. I'm not tall but not short, five feet eleven inches from the flat of my feet to the top of my head to be exact. I run several miles several times a week, so I'm physically fit. My clothes don't sag on my lean frame the way other teenager's seem to. I don't strive to be fit. It is just something that I like doing, running that is. It is simply what I do.

Where I live, there is no park or a smooth running track nearby. There is not even a sidewalk to run on. No, I live in a very rural area of The Palmetto State. There is not a town within ten miles of us.

A lot of the houses that were built here were done so because of the old saw-blade factory. The factory brought a scattering of new people to the area back in the 1920's, but it closed its doors decades ago, putting an end to any potential growth. A lot of the people that came here to work tried to sell their houses after the factory shut down, but few did. Many of them were stuck.

I hate for people to refer to where I live as *the middle of nowhere*. I love it here.

The unlined, old, asphalt road is where I run. Nobody else does it. *Nobody*. When I run, I'm absolutely alone. That is what I like about it. It is glorious. It is simply me and the open air. There will occasionally be a log truck or diesel pickup that passes by, but usually it is just me, alone on the road with my thoughts. I like to go out as the sun is just beginning to set. By the time that I get back home, the sky is my favorite color, that deep blue indigo just before nightfall. It reminds me of the state flag.

In fact, on the day when this story begins, that is what I was doing. I was running.

I had just gotten home from school and flung my backpack onto the floor of my room. Momma and Daddy were not home from work yet. Both of them, Daddy especially, worked a lot. He worked at one of the big banks in town, and Momma was a store manager of a clothing store all the way over in Columbia, which was an hour away. Most of the time she had to work nights and weekends.

I changed into my running clothes and shoes and let Gravel out into the back yard. Gravel was my old white and brown hound dog. There was an old, dead plant from two Christmas's earlier that had a faded red bow wrapped around its pot that he usually peed on, and that day was no exception.

After letting Gravel back in, I petted him on the top of his head, right between the ears. I watched him waddle to the old dog bed that sits on the floor in the corner. The bed had been given to him on the day that he was brought to live with us.

We live in a small, two bedroom house that is located down a dirt road. There is nothing fancy or spectacular about our house. The yard is mostly dirt with a few patches of grass here and there. There is an old tire swing hanging from the big pecan tree that stands in the front yard. The tire swing had been there since I was little. The tire is from my grandfather's old pickup. There are a couple of concrete planters on the front porch, but nothing is in them except dry potting soil. In the backyard there is a small night-garden that I planted myself.

The red dirt driveway is short, and it only takes a few seconds for me to reach the mailbox that is stuck catawampus near the ditch. I made a left onto the dirt road that we live on, Nesting Lane. If I were to go to the right instead of the left it would simply dead-end into an overgrown and unused piece of land that used to be a cow pasture.

Tall trees line both sides of the narrow road. There are pines and oaks. The red clay was packed and felt solid beneath my feet. There are ditches on each side of the road that sometimes have stagnant water standing in the bottom. Usually dragonflies and other insects hover around the water, but on that day there were none because it was so dry. It had been over a month since we had gotten any rain. I went about a quarter of a mile until I came to another house.

Abandoned Manor—that's what we call it.

It is a large, two story, antebellum home that sits on the corner of Nesting Lane and the main road, Highway 378. It's made of brick and has white trim work. Among the several ancient magnolias that grow on the property, there is an enormous live oak that has beautifully twisted, drooping limbs. Across the front of the house there are six white columns that stand from the ground all the way to the roof.

I know that the construction is antebellum because of the history classes that I have taken over the years. The house has been pointed out by several of my teachers as being a prime example of that style of architecture. The columns, the two porches, one of which stretches across the entire second story, the symmetry of the front, the perfectly centered entranceway, and the elaborate friezes that are above the doors and windows are all common characteristics of that architectural style.

No one has lived in the house for as long as I can remember, hence the name—Abandoned Manor. Legend has it that the place is haunted by a girl that lived there back in the 1920s or 30s. I think that her family was associated with the factory in some shape or form.

Now, you might be wondering if I'm afraid of living near an abandoned house that is supposed to be haunted. No, not really. I've never seen anything spooky around there myself. Also, let me set the record straight here. The picture that you probably have in your head at the mention of the house being haunted is more than likely one of a dilapidated structure, busted windows, an open door swinging to and fro, an overgrown lawn, and years of vine growth creeping up the sides of the house.

If so, you're wrong.

The only thing that I find out of the ordinary, despite it being not lived in for so long, is that both the yard and the house are picture perfect. The lawn is healthy green and neatly mowed. Even under the abundant shade of the oak tree, the grass that grows around the large, exposed roots is vibrant. The flower beds and perimeters of the magnolia trees are thick with dark mulch. Azalea bushes bloom all around the property in the spring. During the summer months, none of the flowers are ever droopy with thirst. It is always picture perfect. It is the kind of place that you could imagine sitting in the swing on the front porch, watching lightning bugs as they move about the darkening sky.

There is one light at the house that is always on. The light is on the porch, right next to the front door. It is not that sickening fluorescent or LED that is so common today. Instead, it is a soothing and welcoming yellow.

After passing by Abandoned Manor, I turned west onto the main road. I ran past more trees and similar ditch banks. My feet pounded on the dark pavement of the road.

The road hasn't been paved in years so there are the occasional pot holes and dips in the surface. Like many rural roads, this one is unlined.

I ran about a mile until I came to another house. This one is in stark contrast to Abandoned Manor. The ramshackle cottage belongs to a man named Boston.

Boston is not his real name. It's Frank, but many, many years ago he moved here from Boston, Massachusetts and was given the nickname. The name stuck, and that's what he has been called ever since. Boston lives alone. His wife died before I was born. He has a son and a daughter, twins, but both of them moved away after graduating high school and never came back.

Boston was out in his front yard that day.

Earlier, the day had been warm and sunny, but, by then, it was turning seasonably cool.

It was nearing the end of September and all around Crow County there were festive scarecrows and fall scenes that had been popping up in front of people's houses. There were old wheelbarrows that were full of pumpkins and bulbous gourds that had been parked in front of hay bales and dry corn stalks.

Dove hunting season had just arrived and the next morning would surely bring the pop of hunting rifles all across the area.

Halloween was right around the corner.

The sky was orange from the disappearing sun.

Boston was working in the flower beds that he kept tidy in front of his house. He looked up from his work and waved his garden-gloved hand at me as I passed. I waved back.

From there, after I passed Boston's house, it wasn't long until I heard the first sound of distant sirens. I kept running, but the sirens grew louder quickly. It was only a moment later before two cop cars flew by me in a panicked rush.

It is not often that police cars are seen where we live, so the sound and sight of them sent my nerves racing. My heart was pounding and didn't begin to ease until the cars ventured further up the road and finally out of sight.

I continued running until I came to the sharp curve in the road. It was where I usually turned around. It was roughly one and a half miles from our house. There is a dirt path that leads off to the right, through the brush, and just into the edge of the line of trees. It is where I venture off of the pavement. I had done this so many times over those past several months. It was a familiarity that comforted me.

There was a tallish tree stump from an old oak that I used to stretch my legs on. I remember learning in grade school that the age of any tree could be determined by counting the rings. The rings on this one were too many to count.

From there, I could see Nan's house through the trees. It stands on a large, grassy lot down a long, dirt drive. Nan's family owned a nursery. Several greenhouses are lined along the back of the old farmhouse. Usually, as I stretched, I peered into the yard, hoping to get a glimpse of her. That day, as I looked up, my heart dropped.

The cop cars were in front of their house. Their blue lights were still flashing but the sirens had been turned off. One of the driver's side doors had been left open. I found this to be particularly alarming. To me, it was a sign that the police had been in too much of a hurry to even do something as simple as shutting the door.

My eyes darted from the car to the house, and to the greenhouses and the ground. I saw a vibrant red color spread across the driveway. At first I thought it was blood that had been splattered across the dirt. My eyes shot around again. The center greenhouse door was standing wide open. My heart was hammering in my chest. Something bad had happened. Really bad. I knew this was true without a doubt. That was when I realized that the red I saw in the driveway wasn't blood. It was a scattering of rose petals.

Deep down, I knew, right at that very moment, that what all of us had been afraid of for the past several months had already happened.

The serial killer had finally made his way to Crow County.

3.

five months earlier…

"WELL, I THINK all of this sucks!" Nandina Bush said from the passenger seat of the moving truck. "It's the end of the school year," she said again for what was about the hundredth time. "How would you like to be transplanted to a new school right before your senior year?"

Her mother, Rose Bush, sat across from Nandina with both of her hands gripped around the steering wheel so tightly that her knuckles were turning white. Rose was wearing a pair of large, aviator-style sunglasses. Her black hair was pulled back in a loose ponytail. Even with the glasses, the bright spring sun that tore into the windshield was nearly blinding. "Nan, please don't be so dramatic. What we're doing is a good thing."

Rose thought about what Nandina had said and realized that, from her daughter's standpoint, her statement had absolutely been right. It did suck. What teenager would want to leave all of their friends and home behind just after the end of their junior year?

In the fall, Nan would be a senior and Rose wondered if it wouldn't have been easier to just wait until she graduated to make the move. These thoughts and questions had kept Rose up at night too many times. It would have been so easy just to wait.

Rose reminded herself it was what they needed to do. It was the future for all three of them that she and her husband were thinking about. It was something that they had been planning for a long time, and she was wise enough to know that opportunities didn't just pop up all the time.

It hadn't been but a few months since Rose had spotted the listing for the property on the internet, hidden among what most people would consider much more desirable postings. A home, a business, and several acres of land—it was too good to be true. After talking it over with Tom, they jumped at the chance. From there, everything had moved at the speed of light.

Rose and her husband, Tom, had been in the plant business for a couple of decades by then. So far, they had worked with other farmers and nursery owners. They had started a small business several years back, but what they were doing now was different. This was big. Before, they had sold their plants at farmer's markets, their own little roadside stand, and the garden shows around the area, but now...now they would have an entire greenhouse as their own—three of them in fact.

The truck rattled over the old road.

Rose glanced into the rearview mirror and saw that the second truck, this one being driven by Tom, was right behind them. He was smiling. Below the bill of his cap, he saw his wife glance at him, and he waved out of the open window. Rose smiled back.

"Besides," Rose said and shrugged her shoulders, turning her attention back to her daughter, "you're not that far from your friends. You could see them on the weekends or over the summer..."

Nandina cut her off. "Mom, we've been driving two hours. I doubt that anybody would want to come all the way out here just to hang out." She turned her head and watched the passing landscape.

In reality, she didn't really have that many close friends; it was only two now that Jackson was out of the picture.

Long ago, the moving trucks had turned off the main highway and had been traveling down the back roads for a while. On each side of them, tall pine and oak trees reached up to the blue sky. Below the trees was a bramble of overgrown vegetation—weeds, briars, and that kind of thing. And then, below the plants, much of the ground was made of the hard, red dirt that, in certain places, seemed to be cut at sharp angles by a large carving knife. The red clay was something unfamiliar to the Bushes. They were used to the sogginess of the swampland that was around their home in Bishopville.

"Oh look!" Nan said and pointed through her window. "A house!" she said sarcastically. It was the first that they had seen in several miles. "I wonder who lives there. I guess, by the process of elimination, they'll be my friend."

The old house that they were passing by was amazing.

But as Nandina stared at the beautiful architecture, something else caught her eye. Just ahead of them, there was movement. Someone was running. It was a boy who, from behind, appeared to be about the same age as her. He was wearing a pair of running shorts, a t-shirt, and a cap. Nandina thought that he was cute, and, with her phone held discreetly next to the window, she snapped a picture.

Rose caught what her daughter was doing. "Nandina!" She spoke in a shocked tone at the audacity of her daughter's action, but then laughed at the teenage absurdity of it all. Rose, herself, could remember what it had been like being that age. "So let me guess, now you like the idea of moving out here," she joked.

"Mom!" Nandina shot her mother a look that visualized her deep-set embarrassment. By the time that she turned to look back in the mirror, the running boy was so far in the distance that she couldn't make out any of his features.

Pretty soon, the truck turned off the road and onto the long, dirt drive that led to their new home. The pathway was blocked by a rusty chain that stretched from one post to another. In the corner, near the road, there was an old, weather-worn sign for the greenhouses. The sign was hanging by one chain. The once white paint was chipped and peeling. Vines had wrapped themselves around the posts. It was very cliché, but a large black crow that had been perched on the top corner of the sign took flight.

"You have got to be kidding me," Nandina mumbled under her breath.

With the added effect of the crow, it felt like she had wandered onto the set of a horror movie.

After putting the truck in park, Rose swung her door open, jumped out, and walked around to where she unclasped the chain so that they could drive through.

From inside the cab, and since the driver's side door had been left open, Nandina could hear the rattling of the chain as she watched her mother pull it off to the side and out of the way. Nandina opened the photo album on her phone, selected the picture of the running boy, and typed up a quick message to accompany the shot.

Moving out here just got 100 times better :)

With her right thumb, she hit send.

IN THE FAR back bedroom of a little pea-green cottage, Mala Mujer's phone dinged with the arrival of the incoming message.

She was sitting at an antique, cherry-wood desk that was pushed up against the room's only window. Her laptop was open in front of her. The screen held the work-in-progress manuscript of a romantic novella that she was determined to finish that summer.

Whenever Mala sat at the old piece of furniture that had once belonged to her grandmother, she had a good view of the backyard vegetable garden and flower beds that her mother worked on so diligently. The scene gave her a sense of calm and inspiration.

Mala picked up the phone and immediately saw the photo and text that had come from her best friend. She tapped the photo so that it was larger and then swiped her fingers across the screen, zooming in closer on the boy's features and physique. Like Nandina, she liked what she saw.

Mala typed a reply.

I think you'll be just fine!

Staring through the window at the new tomato plants that had been placed in neat, perfectly aligned rows just a couple of weeks earlier, Mala thought about how much she was going to miss having Nandina around. The two girls had been best friends their entire lives, due to the fact that their mothers had always held a close bond with one another.

In a framed photo that sat on the mantel in the Mujer's living room, Rose Bush and Josephine Mujer stood side by side in front of the tall, carefully shaped plants of Pearl Fryar's Topiary Garden. Both of the women had the enormous, rounded bellies of pregnancy. They wore loose fitting sundresses—Josephine in blue and Rose in yellow. Their complexions were opposite from one another. While Rose was pale and fair, Josephine's skin was the color of black walnuts. The spring sun shone down on them, casting them in a warm glow. In the picture, they looked close to what Mala and Nandina would feel like when they stuffed their own bellies full of the sweet and juicy, vine-ripened watermelon of late summertime—happy and nearly ready to pop.

The love of plants seemed to be a constant thread among both families. It was what had forged the friendship between Rose and Josephine when they had been young and newly married. The Bushes grew and sold plants, while the Mujers, on the other hand, had a history of using herbs and plants for home remedies and, as some people around the area speculated, for performing magic.

After her mother got married to David Mujer and became pregnant shortly thereafter, Josephine had been so enchanted by the idea that Rose had named her daughter Nandina Bush. When she discovered that there was a plant called Mala Mujer, she nearly caused David's heart to jump out of his throat when she called him in a whirlwind of excitement. "I thought something was wrong," David laughed whenever he told the story. "She sounded like the house was burning down!"

"I was named after a weed," Mala would often say whenever the story was brought up.

It was true. Mala Mujer is a poisonous weed that is native to desert climates. A common name for it is Bad Woman.

But Mala hadn't always held a certain amount of disdain for her name.

When Mala and Nandina were in grade school, they would often go with their mothers to visit the same Bishopville garden that was in the photo on the mantel.

Many of the topiaries in the garden were started from plants that had been thrown away. Mr. Fryar, the gardener, trimmed the bushes and trees into circles, squares, elaborate designs, and even the word *Love*.

Mala and Nandina would wander off by themselves where they would imagine the different things that the tall, carefully shaped bushes and trees could be. Back then, they had been enchanted with the idea of being named after plants; no matter that one of them was an unwanted weed. To the girls, because of their names, it seemed like they were destined to be friends. In their young imagination, they would often wonder how likely and magnificent would it be to find a husband that also had the name of a plant.

Then the teenage years came rushing in like a herd of goats, and the idea lost its romantic luster. From thirteen on, they would laugh about the childish fairy tales that Mala had written in her room late at night. "It would never happen," Mala would say. "What in the world was I ever thinking? The chances of running into a boy with a name like that are slim to none."

4.

SO YEAH, IT was me that Nan saw from where she sat in the passenger seat of the moving truck that day. I mean, it doesn't take a rocket scientist to understand that little tidbit. And no, I didn't know about the picture. I didn't find out about that until later.

Thinking back on it now, I couldn't believe that it had only been five months between the day that she and her parents had moved to Crow County and the time of Rose getting attacked. So much had happened in such a short period of time. *Too much.*

By then, I mean the day of the attack, we had known for months that there was a serial killer roaming the state. How could we not? It was all over the news. Up until the day that it happened to

Rose, I hadn't really worried that much about it. Even though I knew that the killer was somewhere out there, I didn't think that my life would ever be in danger because of him or her. I couldn't begin to comprehend the possibility that such a horrendous crime could happen to someone that I knew. I couldn't even fathom the far-reaching effects that it would have on all of us.

What I knew about the situation was that someone was killing people that shared their names with plants and that at each crime scene there had been a scattering of flowers left behind.

That was how I knew, before it had even been confirmed by the local law enforcement, that the killer had struck that day. The red rose petals told me all I needed to know. It was the killer's calling card.

Rose Bush.

I remember how I felt when my mind registered what I was seeing through the trees that day.

I was already breathing heavily and had high adrenaline from completing half of my three-mile run, but when I saw the rose petals strewn across the ground, my heart nearly beat through my ribcage. There was a steady trail of them that led all the way from the middle greenhouse to the dirt driveway.

The killer was immediately what I thought about. Fear clenched me.

Then I saw her—Rose—lying face down on the ground. She wasn't moving. One of her arms, I think it was her right, was stretched straight out over her head. The other arm was twisted underneath her abdomen. Both of her legs were bent at the knees. It was strange; she was wearing a nice, black dress, like the kind that she would wear if she were going out somewhere. From where I stood, I could see a pool of red rose petals that was spread out in what looked like a spray of blood that originated from where her head rested on the dirt of the driveway.

For some reason, the dirt is something that I can recall in such clarity that it is confusing as to why it stands out so much to me. That day, the dirt was dry. Everything was. By then we had gone weeks without rainfall, and, up until the past few days, the weather had been blisteringly hot. It was the time of year where summer was just beginning to slip into fall, and frost was right around the corner. But even with the promise of cooler temperatures, that year, despite the longer nights and shorter days, summer seemed to want to hold onto us as long as possible.

When I think about what happened to Rose, and when I have nightmares about it, one of the details that I see every time is a thick cloud of dust that rises up from all around her body when it hits the ground.

Something else I remember about that day was the deep rooted fear that I felt as I stood alone at the edge of the woods watching the events unfolding down the slope from me. This deep feeling of fear overcame me immediately.

As I stood alone at the edge of the woods, and the reality of what I was seeing began to sink in I realized it was very likely that the killer could be just a few steps away from where I stood. I remember thinking, I can't leave here and go home by myself. What if the killer is still out here?

I looked around at my surroundings. The inside of the woods was getting darker by the second. The shadows of the trees were long and reached over me. I could hear movement behind me. I think now that what I heard was probably just the feet of some small animal—a mouse or a squirrel searching for a fallen acorn or berry—but in that single, horrifying moment, everything I heard was the sound of a psychopath.

I stepped out of the trees and began to walk down the incline onto the Bush's property. As much as this shames me, and has become a realization that haunts me to this day, I'll admit it, I wasn't going toward them to help with the situation. I was going toward the police for my *own* protection, to simply be near another person. I was that scared.

After just a few steps, I remember seeing one of the cops noticing me and saying something to his partner who immediately spun her head in my direction. Both of them instinctively reached for their guns. I realize now that I must've looked like a walking nightmare to them as I unexpectedly emerged from the darkness. Looking back on it now, I realize that they must have surely thought that I was the perp. I'm still amazed that I didn't get shot that day.

But I didn't.

And Rose didn't die in her driveway on that late September evening.

Not long after I had begun trekking down the embankment with both of my hands held up high over my head in a posture of unarmed innocence, I could hear the siren from another vehicle approaching from behind me.

The ambulance sped past just as I was emerging from long shadows of the trees and wheeled into the driveway. As the ambulance bounced over the deeply rutted driveway, behind it, a thick cloud of dust rose into the sky. The ambulance stopped at the scene.

One of the police officers turned his attention away from me and said something to the driver.

From where I was descending the embankment, I watched the paramedics jump out and place Rose onto a stretcher which they immediately rolled into the back of the ambulance. With its lights flashing, and Rose being transported in the back, the ambulance sped away from the scene.

I was left alone with the police officers, both of which had their handguns pointed at me once again.

SINCE THE SMALL county hospital closest to us didn't have an intensive care unit, Rose had been sent all the way to Columbia.

Everything about the city was so vastly different from where I had lived. Even though it had been the middle of the morning when I drove myself to the hospital, the traffic on the roads through the city were bumper to bumper.

I can't imagine dealing with the sounds of the city every day. Even from deep within the corridors of the hospital I could hear the cacophony of city life on the other side of the walls. I could hear the hectic rush of the steady, unrelenting traffic. There was the occasional angry blow of car horns. I was amazed that the traffic seemed to never die down. In the city, people always seemed to have somewhere they needed to go.

I sat hunched over in an incredibly uncomfortable chair in the corner of the room. Nan sat next to me on what was surely an equally painful futon. Her eyes were bloodshot from crying and she had dark bags under them from both the lack of sleep and worry that she had been forced to contend with. She wasn't wearing shoes and her sock covered feet were pulled up underneath her bottom. I remember that the socks she had on that day were pink. Rumpled white sheets were between her and the futon cushions from where Tom had slept the night before. Tom wasn't there then. He had just stepped out for a cup of coffee and promised that he would be right back.

Across from us, in the center of the room, Rose was lying on her back. Her eyes were closed. Various tubes and IVs had been stuck into her. They snaked out of the back of her hands and her nose. In stark contrast to the scariness of the medical equipment, vases of soft, colorful flowers stood on the side table next to her. I recognized them as being peonies and laurel.

By then Rose hadn't even been in the hospital for twenty four hours. Since the attack, she had been unconscious and completely nonresponsive. I remember thinking, if only she could talk, if only she could give a description of the killer.

But if she *could* talk, then what would happen next?

Maybe the cops would have more of an idea of who they were looking for. Maybe *we* would know more of who to be cautious of. As far as we knew, the killer could've been anybody.

What was even scarier was the idea that it could've been somebody that I knew.

I felt like all eyes were on us. It had turned into a media circus. On every local station, the nightly, morning, and midday news was covered in the tragedy that we were unfortunate to be in the midst of. It felt surreal to be living dead center in the crazy events that were unfolding all around us.

The Killer is Here!, one local headline read. *Crow County Horror*, another proclaimed. *Plant Killer Strikes Again!*

Even at that moment, I looked out of the large window of the hospital room and saw that the news trucks were lined up on the dark pavement near the edge of the building. Of course the security staff of the hospital wouldn't let the reporters inside, but outside it was free game. It was like they were hunters waiting on their prey to emerge from the sliding glass doors, and sadly we were the ones that were being hunted.

Since Rose's attempted murder, the local news programs had been recapping the details so far in the Plant Killer case. Rose had been the first victim to survive an attack by the perpetrator. And since she had survived, it wasn't just *us* that were waiting for her to regain consciousness; everyone was waiting with baited breath for her to speak. The news people wanted more than anything to be there when this happened. Every reporter hoped to be the one to cover the breaking story. The general public wanted to know immediately what her first words were going to be. Her coma had the entire state checking for updates via the internet every chance they got.

Her survival wasn't the only thing that was different from the other victims either. All the others had been stabbed repeatedly with a sharp blade, presumably some sort of gardening tool. Rose, on the other hand, had no other blood or stab wounds found anywhere on her body.

Comas can be caused by several things. Some infections can become so severe that it causes the person to fall into a comatose state. Drugs and alcohol can be a contributing factor. A person can be poisoned. Even certain plants, when ingested, have the ability to shut the brain down. Sometimes comas are medically induced to prevent swelling of the brain and causing even further damage than what was already started.

Rose's situation was because she had been bludgeoned. The doctor told us that it was undeniably a blow to the head that had knocked her unconscious and placed her into the coma. With this revelation, and the lack of stab wounds, many assumed that the killer had changed his method of attack. People speculated that it was very possible that the Plant Killer's future victims would more than likely suffer a strike to the head instead of being stabbed. This was talked about by both the local law enforcement and the blonde news anchors that sat behind the sleek soundstage desks.

Earlier that day, I had watched in horror as a young, perky reporter stood outside of the Bush's property. The greenhouses and the old farmhouse stood behind her. Yellow crime scene tape was stretched across the driveway.

"It was here at Bush's Greenhouses, located just off Highway 378 in Crow County, where it is believed that the most recent attack by the *Plant Killer* took place early yesterday evening."

The camera zoomed in on the house. There was both a red, white, and blue American flag and a South Carolina state flag that hung from the posts that flanked the wide front steps. This was an image that the media loved. It showed that bad things could happen in a place as quaint as Crow County. On the looped video there was a close up of each of the greenhouses and then one of the sign that stood by the road. By then the sign that Nan had seen on the day that she had arrived had been repaired. It now hung with two chains and had a fresh coat of white paint. BUSH'S GREENHOUSES & NURSERY, it read.

Seeing it on TV was sickening. Being miles away and watching our home be broadcast on the news to anyone that wanted to see made it seem invasive. It made what we were going through feel even more surreal. I wanted more than anything for none of this to have ever happened.

Since then, the wall mounted TV of the hospital room had been turned off. We simply hadn't been able to watch anymore. The story was everywhere we looked, and watching it only added to our paranoia and fear. And truth be told, it was me and Nan that had the most to be afraid of. We were the ones that had the names that could be our doom.

I glanced over at Nan. There was a cross that hung from a silver chain around her neck that I had given her. She was twirling the pendant between her fingers and she had a faraway look in her eyes. I knew that the fear that she felt for her mother far outweighed everything else, but when it came down to it, the possibility of being the next victim was a reality for both of us. Believe me—I had already searched the internet for others. I just wanted to assure myself that the other people that I loved would be safe from the nightmare. To my relief there was not a plant called a Thomas Bush or a Clarissa or Bradley Miller. But because of our names, mine and Nan's, I knew that we could easily be next on the killer's list.

THE DOOR TO the hospital room opened and Tom came in. He was carrying a cup of coffee. I knew him well enough to know that the coffee inside the disposable cup was black. It was the way that he liked it.

I could tell just by looking at him that he was frazzled beyond belief. His thin, brown hair was still matted down from when he had removed his cap several hours earlier. It was obvious that he hadn't taken a shower since everything had happened. His eyes were bloodshot. I remember how terrible I felt for him. I couldn't imagine what it would be like to be in his position.

There was someone with him. At first, from where I sat on the futon next to Nan, all I saw was the abrupt movement of arms inside of a blue jacket behind Tom, but then I registered the face that I was seeing. It was Colby, Tom's younger brother.

Nan stood up as soon as she saw her father and uncle enter the room.

Colby walked over to her and wrapped her in his arms.

"I got here as soon as I could," he said.

Colby lived in Bishopville. He was the uncle that Nan had stayed with while she had finished out the school year back in April and May.

Colby turned to me and smiled. He reached out his hand and squeezed my shoulder in a gesture of assuring me that everything would be okay.

As he, Tom, and Nan talked, I felt my phone vibrating in my pocket. I had turned the ringer off since going into the hospital earlier that day. When I pulled it out of my jeans pocket, I saw that there was a text from Momma.

We're on our way there. You can ride home with your dad, and I'll drive your truck. We don't want you to travel alone. We've made arrangements for you to stay at Bartley's house until all of this is over. XO

Bartley Vance and I had been friends our entire lives, but lately we hadn't been hanging out as much as we used to. It wasn't because of the fact that he had dated my ex-girlfriend; that kind of thing happens around here all the time. I mean, when there are only so many people in the area that are around your age, at some point in time you are bound to go out with the same girl.

Bartley's a year older than me and graduated back in the spring. Since then, he had been hanging out with the older guys that he worked with at his father's real-estate company.

The reason that I didn't really want to stay at his house was because of the fact that his parents were planning a huge eighteenth birthday party for him that weekend. With everything else that was going on, I wasn't in the mood for a party.

I texted her back.

What? Why?

It only took a minute for Momma to reply.

Dusty, their house will be much safer than ours, and it is what the police suggested for us to do. They said not to tell ANYBODY where you are.

As much as I hated the idea of staying at Bartley's house, I knew that they were just looking out for my own good. There was, after all, a serial killer on the loose. And she was right. Bartley's house would surely be safer than ours. His dad had their house sealed up like a tomb. The entire property was fenced in with a tall, brick wall. An enormous, iron gate that you had to have a code to open stood at the entrance to the dark, paved driveway. Not only were the doors and windows outfitted with the best security alarms that money could buy, but they were also the type of glass that you can't break. On top of all that, he had security cameras that routinely scanned the property and a cabinet full of guns in the living room. Sometimes I wondered what he was so afraid of.

When it was time for me to go, Nan walked me to the door. We stepped into the hallway. A nurse walked by us and smiled. By then, visiting hours were over and we were the only three people in the hallway. Nan and I hugged. I could smell the shampoo in her hair. I didn't want to leave her, but, in a way, I knew that she was safer in the hospital than she would be back at home.

As terrible as the hospital had been, in a way, it was a safe place.

"I hope they catch whoever did this," Nan said. "I can't stand not knowing."

I nodded in agreement. "They'll figure it out," I told her.

We broke away from one another, and after I began walking away, I looked over my shoulder at her one more time.

5.

AS YOU KNOW, Nan wasn't the first of her family to be named after a plant. She wasn't even the second.

Before Rose married Tom and became *Rose Bush*, Nandina's grandmother had been Lily Lavallée by marriage. According to Nan, *Lavallée* is a French word that means *of the valley*. After getting married, and up until the end of her life, her grandmother would tell people every chance she got that she was *Lily of the Valley*. It was a joke among the family that Lily married Sgt. William Lavallée, Jr. just so she could have the unique surname.

Soon after becoming Mrs. Lavallée, Lily gave birth to a baby girl that she and her husband named Rose. The Lavallée family had a small sun-garden behind their house where they grew yellow lilies and roses that hinted at the color of the sun. As a child, Rose loved playing in the sun-garden. It was where her interest in plants began. As she got older and found out that she could make a living doing what she loved, the path toward her future was set in stone.

Rose met Tom in college. She was surprised to discover that his interest in horticulture seemed to rival hers, and they quickly fell in love. When they were married, she became Rose Bush.

So, unlike me, Nandina's parents knew *exactly* what they were doing when they named her. Her full name is Nandina Bush. They thought it was cute.

The plants are a type of bamboo that comes from the scientific genus name of Berberidaceae. Nandina bushes are hearty, thriving plants that are considered to be invasive by many people. In Florida, they are actually on the most invasive pest plant list. In the late fall and winter months, they are covered in clusters of red or white berries. Some of the leaves are green, while at times, many of them can be tinted a purplish crimson. The berries are poisonous. More on that later.

WE HAD HEARD rumors of the greenhouses being sold throughout the first part of the year. Whispers of who, what, and when spread faster than a bell clapper in a goose's ass, as Gran would say.

That January had been cold. In fact, many nights had even reached all time record lows. It was the one time in my life when I'd seen Pritchard's Pond freeze over into a solid sheet of ice. The air was so frigid that the idea of someone opening up the greenhouses and selling fresh, young plants filled us all with hope; it gave us a promise of a new spring and summer just when we needed it the most.

The greenhouses and the old farmhouse had stood vacant for as long as I could remember. From what I had been told, the last people that lived at the house and ran the business had moved away from the area in the late eighties.

When the FOR SALE sign that had stood out on Highway 378 for years had been marked as SOLD, people began to get even more curious.

Since we only lived down the road from the greenhouses, on Sundays after church, people would often ask *us* if we had heard anything about the new owners.

The church that we go to is called Crow Baptist. It stands at an intersection just a couple of miles from our house. It is in the opposite direction from the Bush's greenhouses.

In the winter, when I stood on our back porch, I could easily see the steeple of the church through the bare tree limbs of the woods that separated us.

After that particular week's sermon, we were gathered in small groups in the parking lot of the church, just as we usually did. I was with Momma, Daddy, Gran, and an old lady named Catherine.

Catherine lived on the edge of town. She always had her nose in other people's business. She had heavy, black framed glasses and blue hair. Not the *I'm so cool, look at me* kind of hipster blue, but steel blue. Hers was that color because of the special wash that Catherine and a lot of the other old women tended to get at the salon.

All around us was the sound of blackbirds. The avian calls seemed to travel endlessly in the winter. Under the bleak and gray February sky, I remember standing to the side and only halfway listening to Momma's and Daddy's conversation with Catherine. She asked if we had met our new neighbors.

"No, not yet, but somebody said that they were Bushes," Momma said.

"You think they're any kin to Loretta Bush?" Catherine asked.

Momma shook her head. "I don't think so," she said. "It seems like somebody would have already mentioned that."

And they weren't. They were not related to anyone in Crow County. It isn't often that a family with no ties to the area moves to where we live. As I've said before, since the saw-blade factory had shut down decades earlier, there isn't much out here in the way of work. So, if you weren't born and bred here, the place doesn't draw much interest from the outside, but, at the time, the Bushes just happened to be in the market for buying a large plot of land with three greenhouses. For them it was perfect. All the stars seemed to have aligned at just the right time.

Crow County is situated just to the left of the center of the state. Where we live is nothing but rural land. We are fifteen miles from the town of Crow. When I step outside of my house in the morning, it is earthy things that I smell instead of car exhaust and greasy fast food joints. The only noise that I hear is that of nature with the occasional chainsaw, truck, or four-wheeler mixed in with it.

The same people have been living around me my entire life. That is why we all took the arrival of the Bushes with a form of curious excitement, and, I must admit, a tad bit of trepidation.

I vividly remember the day that I saw the moving trucks pass by me while I was out on my morning run. It was the beginning of April, two months after the gossip in the church parking lot. We were out of school for spring break that week. By then, the weather had turned warm, and there was a coat of yellow pollen on everything. The pink and white azaleas around Abandoned Manor were in full bloom. The grass surrounding the property had already moved out of the dormancy of winter and was the vibrant green of fresh parsley and basil.

There were two trucks that approached and passed me from behind. I didn't see either of the drivers, Tom or Rose. I didn't catch my first glimpse of Nan that day, but, just by the sight of the trucks, I knew that it was them. It was the people that we had heard and speculated about.

A few days later, while Daddy was at work, Momma spent some of the morning making a homemade pie to take to our new neighbors. The pie was made out of strawberries that she had picked up at the market earlier in the week. The strawberry pies that she made had a latticed crust across the top that allowed the sticky red syrup from the berries to bubble through.

I rode with her. I'm not sure why I agreed to go, but, thinking back on it now, I realize that it was out of sheer nosiness. It is a trait that most Southerners tend to have.

At the old, lopsided sign for the greenhouses, Momma steered the car off 378 and onto the long, sparsely graveled drive that led to the house. The beginning of the driveway was bushy and overgrown on both sides with trees that were in dire need of trimming, but the rutted path quickly opened up into a beautiful expanse of open land that was surrounded on all sides by dense woods. It was the first time that I can ever remember actually *being* on the property and not just seeing it from the road. It was a large clearing in the middle of the Crow County woods. A handful of large pecan and walnut trees dotted the land. Other than those trees, the land was a stretch of green. The grass was so tall that it swayed in the light breeze. From the lazy blue sky, the spring sun added a golden hue.

The two story house that sat on the land looked exactly like what most people would picture when they hear the word *farmhouse*. With its aged, clapboard siding, a tin roof that had a forty-five degree pitch, old screen doors, and wide front porch, it was a glorious and comforting stereotype.

We parked in the circular drive and walked side by side across the yard. We went up the front steps, across the width of the porch, and up to the front door. The main door was standing open, leaving only the screen door between us and the inside. It was the type of beautifully constructed screen door that you would see propped up against the wall in an antique store. The cutout in the upper portion of the door was in the shape of a large oval and the bottom was a horizontal row of railed slats.

On the other side of the screen, there was a short hallway that had a door on each side that led to other rooms. I could see that the end of the hallway opened up into a larger space where there was an old cabinet that was against the wall that faced the front door. There was a single candle that was flickering on top of the cabinet.

I could hear low music coming from one of the rooms that was inside the house. It was a soft song that had the twang-y vocals that I recognized as belonging to country star, Mandy Walker.

Momma knocked and caused the screen door to shake back and forth within its frame. It was only a moment later when we saw Rose rounding the corner of the hallway.

This was my very first impression of Rose as I watched her through the screen door that day—she was my mother's age, but she was beyond hot. It was the first time that I had ever been in the presence of someone old enough to have given birth to me and wished that I was older. She had long, pitch-black hair. Her skin was milky white. She was wearing jeans and a dirty, white t-shirt, presumably her husband's. The too big t-shirt draped perfectly from her slim shoulders. Her lips were deep red, and she was smiling.

"Hey, we're your neighbors from down the street," Momma said through the screen door. "I'm Clarissa, and this is my son, Dusty."

Rose pushed the door open and introduced herself. To this day, I can still hear the sound that those old hinges made.

"It's so good to meet y'all," she said with a wide smile. "I just met Boston yesterday."

I was surprised that old man Boston had put forth the effort to introduce himself to *anyone*. Not that he's not nice, he is. It's just that people from up North are so different from us. They make jokes about us and our "Southern hospitality" and all, but they like it. I know they do. I guess he's finally catching on to the way we do things around here. For a brief moment, I wondered if he had brought the Bushes a pie like we had.

"How old are you Dusty?"

Rose was looking at me and I felt my cheeks ignite.

"Seventeen," I said and my voice cracked. I was embarrassed by the juvenile reaction.

"Our daughter turns seventeen next month. I guess the two of you'll be in the same grade."

She explained to us that instead of transferring schools that close to the end of the term, her daughter would be staying at an uncle's house in Bishopville to finish up the school year. On the weekends she would be there with them at the new house.

Rose stepped aside and held the door open with her outstretched arm. "Y'all come in for a minute."

"Oh, I don't want to intrude. I know you must be busy unpacking and everything else that comes with moving into a new house. I just wanted to come by and introduce ourselves. Here, I made you a pie."

Smiling, Momma held the pie out in front of her.

"You shouldn't have done that." Rose said with a smile.

"I wanted to." Momma shrugged her shoulders and handed the pie over to Rose. "When do y'all plan on opening?"

I thought that it was funny how she cut right to the chase.

Rose laughed. "Actually, we hope to be up and running by the end of the month. My husband has been working diligently on everything. In fact, let me put this down and I'll take you out there and show you around. He's out there working right now."

She began to turn around to walk back into the house but stopped. She looked over her shoulder at us.

"Come in!" she said again, motioning with her right hand. This time she sounded more insistent.

Momma looked at me and back at Rose. "Just for a minute," she said, sounding defeated.

Rose led us into the house. The screen door slapped shut behind us.

I couldn't believe how bright it was inside. There were large, open windows on each wall. The sunlight reflected off the wide, polished slats of the hardwood floors. The inside of the house smelled like oil soap, floor wax, and the lemon scented candle that was burning at the end of the hallway.

"Ignore the mess," Rose said in reference to the cardboard boxes that were stacked neatly along the floor and had been pushed against the wall and safely out of the way.

And to be honest with you, I was so enamored with the old beauty of the house that I didn't even notice the boxes.

"Have you ever seen the inside of the house before today?" Rose's voice echoed off the solid, empty walls. "I thought, with you living so close, maybe you've been in here before." She had stepped through the doorway on the left that led into the kitchen where she placed the pie on the butcher-block counter top. A white farmhouse sink sat on top of starkly white cabinets.

Momma shook her head. "No, I haven't, but it is beautiful. That's for sure."

"We have a lot of work to do, but I absolutely love it," Rose told us. "Let me show you around."

She gave us a quick tour of the house. She told us that the hardwood floors were the original ones from when the house had been built around 1910, and that as far as she could tell, the kitchen appliances and the claw-foot bathtubs had probably been in the house ever since.

She led us into the back room and up a set of old, wooden stairs that creaked under our feet. There was a large window at the end of the second floor hallway that overlooked the greenhouses and the woods that stood beyond them. The late afternoon sun shone brightly through the uncovered window panes that were the old kind that tend to have waves and imperfections within the glass.

On the second floor were three rooms; it was two bedrooms and a bath. Through the open door of the bathroom, in addition to the black and white ceramic tile on the floor, I caught a quick glimpse of one of the two claw-foot tubs that she had mentioned earlier.

Rose walked across the hall and showed us the master bedroom. The bed was made with white linens. The large window behind the bed had yet to be covered with curtains or blinds. There was an old dresser on each side of the room. Some of Rose's jewelry shimmered on top of one of them.

From there, she led us to the other room that was on the second floor. It was another bedroom. I knew that the room I was about to see must've been *the daughter's*. Even though I didn't know her name at the time, I wanted to take in as much detail about the room as I could. I thought that her personal belongings would give me a better idea about her. So I leaned around Momma, stretched my neck, and peaked around the doorframe.

But what I saw was just nondescript, unpacked boxes, and similar to her parents' room, the bed had been made with plain, white linens. Basically, the contents of the room told me *nothing.*

After showing us the inside of the house, Rose led the two of us back down the stairs and through a door that was at the back of the kitchen. The door opened onto a small, concrete porch that had steps and an iron rail that led into the backyard. Next to the porch, there was an overly thick patch of border grass that was growing against the house.

For some strange reason, I imagined that deep within the grass would be the perfect place to hide an Easter egg. Then, as if I was certain that it had happened before, I wondered how many eggs *had been* hidden there over the years. This simple and seemingly out-of-the-blue thought gave me a soothing idea of the history of the house and the people that had lived there before.

There were a total of three greenhouses on the property. At the time, I didn't know anything about the construction of greenhouses, but I've learned some since then. Actually, I've learned *a lot*. That day, the plastic sides were in tatters. Some of it had come loose from the metal, curved frames and flapped in the light breeze.

It was the one on the far left that Rose led us to. She opened the door and stepped inside. Momma followed her, and I was last. The door was on hinges, and like the door that was on the house, it slapped shut when I slid my hand away. The inside was humid. It smelled like dirt and moisture. Other than two long rows of waist high wooden pallets and a low hanging sprinkler system that was made of copper pipe, the greenhouse was empty.

Mr. Bush was on the far side, near the oscillating fan that was slowly churning the air. He was lifting a stack of what appeared to be old plant trays from the floor.

"Tom," Rose called across the width of the space. "These are our neighbors, Clarissa and her son, Dusty."

Tom placed the trays onto the closest pallet and began walking toward us. He was removing his work gloves one at a time as he walked. His steps were long and assured. By the time he reached us, he was removing the cap from his head. He held out his hand to Momma.

"Nice to meet you, ma'am." He released her hand, turned to me, and held out his hand in my direction. "Nice to me you too," he said.

His handshake was firm and it felt like he could crush every single bone in my hand if he wanted to.

I remember looking into his eyes as his hand firmly held mine. There was a look of determination and assuredness in them. Like Rose, Tom was good looking. I could tell from Momma's face as she stood across from me that she thought the same.

THE NEXT MORNING was when I started running westbound, toward their house. I guess you could say I was being nosy, but really I was doing it in hopes that I would finally see her, the Bush's daughter.

Before that day, I had always run in the opposite direction, toward the church, and had turned around in the empty, paved parking lot.

Back then, on that first day of running toward the Bush's, my turn-around spot at the large oak stump was overgrown. The ground had yet to be trampled numerous times by the soles of my shoes.

Since then, I would run there nearly every day, turning around and stopping to stretch my legs on that stump while scanning the Bush's yard for her.

And finally, through the trees, she was there. At first I thought that it was Rose, but no, it was her, Nandina.

She looked so much like a younger version of her mother that it was nearly unbelievable. That day she was wearing a pair of cut off jean shorts and a blue tank top. Her black hair was pulled back in a ponytail. She was lifting a cardboard box from the back of Tom's pickup and carried it into the house.

Of course, I didn't have the balls to run over there and introduce myself. No way in hell was I brave enough for that. I simply stood from the distance and admired her. I watched.

Okay, I know it sounds kind of creepy and all, but that is what I did. I stood in the trees and watched. And I'm not a creep. I'm just your average, all-American guy. Before her, I had never had a hot girl living so close to me. I see nothing wrong with what I did. If you were me, you would have done the same thing. Don't lie.

I couldn't stop thinking about her that weekend.

Remember when I said that some people consider nandina bushes to be invasive? Well, they're right. From that moment on, and through the remainder of that spring and summer, she was nearly *all* that I could think about.

I finally met her at school the following Monday.

J.H. Academy is named after a Confederate soldier that had been from Crow County, Jasper Holt. The school is not that big. All in all, there are only a couple hundred students. It is a private school with grades K through 12 sharing two buildings. It is very likely, and actually kind of expected, that you'll graduate with the same people that you went to kindergarten with. The same kid that stole your fruit gummies when you were just learning the ins and outs of the world could be sitting next to you twelve years later, wearing a valedictorian sash and smiling big at his or her accomplishments. Even so, there are those occasional new students that transfer in, like Nandina.

She stood in between each of her parents as they made their way down the hallway of the school. Tom and Rose went into the office where they were seeking information about registering and enrolling for the next school year. Nandina stayed in the hallway.

It was early in the morning, and the first bell of the day hadn't even rung yet. There were students rushing all around me trying to get to their homeroom on time. The hallway was full of the sounds of metal locker doors slamming shut and the scratch of vinyl backpacks being slung over shoulders. There was so much going on that the Bushes must not have noticed me standing off to the side in the little alcove that was across from the office. I was next to a large, glass display case of trophies that the sports teams had won over the years.

I watched as several different girls approached Nandina, twirling their blonde and auburn hair around their fingers, obviously trying to get her to join *their* clique. I observed several of the jocks ogle her as they passed by. I liked the way that she didn't pay them any attention, not a single one of them, not even Bartley Vance. For her not to acknowledge *him* was simply astounding.

Bartley was tall and fit. He played sports and did the usual things that the guys around the area were expected to do. He hunted and rode four-wheelers up and down all of the dirt roads. He drank beer on Friday nights and dressed up nice to go to dinner and the movies on Saturday. Every single Sunday morning he was in church. Most of the girls thought that he was perfect. If you were a female at J.H. Academy, when Bartley gave you even a minute of his time, you bowed to him. Just ask Moira. For Nandina not to even *look* in his direction was astounding. It was proof that she really was in a league of her own.

"She's cute," a voice that I immediately recognized said from my left.

Moira Everson, my ex, was facing me. She was wearing an expensive pumpkin-colored blouse. She had long, blonde hair and green eyes. She was perfect.

Moira looked at Nan. "But to be honest with you, I'm still trying to finalize my first impression," she said, "but I guess, if she's nice, you should ask her out." With that, Moira walked away.

My relationship with Moira was admittedly strange. Before she dated me, broke up with me, and then went out with Bartley, we had all been friends. To an outsider, it might have seemed odd for my ex-girlfriend to be giving me relationship advice, but, having known Moira my entire life, it really wasn't that bizarre.

Tom and Rose stepped out of the office, and I saw all three of them glance my way. I quickly spun around and pretended to be looking at the trophies that were lined up in front of me. How stupid is that? I've gone to that school my entire life and had seen those *same* trophies thousands of times. Why would I be looking at them? Like I even cared about any of that stuff anyway.

I could have been named anything in the entire world. Ben, Jason, Ramsey, or Christian, but for whatever reason, I was named Dusty. And it was because of my name that Rose introduced us.

"Dusty?" I heard her say from behind me in the hallway. When I turned around, she was standing just several feet from me. "This is Dusty Miller," she said, looking at her daughter. "He's the one that I was telling you about. He's the one that was also named after a plant." Rose turned her attention back to me. "Dusty, this is our daughter, Nandina Bush."

Nandina was even more striking up close. She was wearing a pair of dark-washed jeans and a loose fitting button-down shirt that was the color of lemon and had little blue flowers printed all over it. Her black hair was loose and hung down past her shoulders.

Nandina smiled and said hello.

And did I see her cheeks begin to blush, or was it only my imagination?

I felt awestruck and frozen in place. I wanted to speak but wasn't able to utter a word. You have to understand that, aside from being nervous about meeting her, there was also a little bit of shame because of how I had been watching her from the woods. Thankfully, Nandina seemed completely unaware of what I had been doing. Finally, the bell rang, forcing a break in the awkwardness that I felt.

"I—uh—it was nice to meet you," I said. "I need to be heading to class." I nodded my head to my right toward nowhere in particular. "See you around?"

"Yeah, I hope so," she told me.

I turned away from the three of them and headed down the hall toward class.

The rest of the day was spent thinking about her. And to be honest with you, I was barely able to even listen to anything that the teachers said. My mind was completely focused on her.

I LOOKED UP the nandina plant on the internet and read everything that I could about it.

Gran laughed when I told her about my newfound horticulture knowledge. I must admit that it felt like I knew something that was gravely important. It seemed like I had stumbled onto some obscure knowledge that no one in Crow County had ever heard of.

"Well, I know all about those butt-ugly bushes, Dusty," Gran said. It was only a week after seeing Nan for the first time. "They spread like crazy and are nearly impossible to get rid of."

We were sitting in her kitchen. It was just me and her. Outside the open window, dusk was already falling.

I vividly remember that evening at Gran's house. The screen door that led to the backyard was standing wide open; the kitchen was full of the scents of a new spring. It smelled like cut grass and freshly bloomed wild flowers. In front of me, a fried bologna sandwich with yellow mustard and cheddar cheese sat on an heirloom, blue ceramic plate.

"I remember when I was growing up, everybody had them. A lot of people planted them around their house just like everyone plants boxwoods nowadays. *This* house had them at one time. Cranky worked blisters all on his hands hoeing and pulling and snipping, trying to get rid of that mess."

Cranky was her husband of over fifty years. His real name was Jack Cranston. He died when I was little, but I remember that he was tall, thin, and muscular. He was always dressed in a white button-down shirt, a pair of suspenders, and jeans. He had a cap that never left his head. Gran said that he even slept in the cap sometimes, much to her chagrin.

The cap was a rather generic mesh-back trucker cap. It was green. The bill was so severely bent and threadbare that it looked like one of the designer ones that the hipsters buy. Cranky's cap was that way from wear and tear. It had earned it's much sought after look.

"There's still some of them growing down by the fence." Gran pointed over my head and through the plaster wall. She was holding a cast iron pan in one hand. "You have some of it at your house too," she said turning her attention back to me.

I bit into the bologna sandwich. I was trying to visualize my own yard and where the bushes could be growing. I realized that I had no idea. I watched as Gran placed the pan on the stovetop and turned the heat on high. Almost immediately, the kitchen was filled with the tantalizing scent of years of bacon grease coming from the much used and cherished cast iron.

After finishing my sandwich, Gran offered me homemade biscuits. I took one, and then she wanted me to eat a piece of cornbread that she had made earlier that day. With the fried bologna and then the biscuit, I was stuffed, but I couldn't resist the offer, so I took a big hunk of it anyway and slathered it with butter.

After eating the cornbread, I stood from the table. The chair legs slid harmoniously against the old linoleum.

"I was just fixin' to fry some fatback for peas later tonight," she said. "Stay for a piece."

I laughed. "I can't. I've got a test tomorrow that I've got to study for. Besides, you've already fed me enough for an army."

"Oh, phooey," she said. "A test in what? There is no way in all of Crow County that it can be more important than a piece of my fatback."

I laughed again. "You're probably right, but I didn't do so great on the last one. And it's in calculus, by the way."

She turned her attention back to the stovetop, and with a fork, she began placing the thick slices of fatback in the pan. The familiar sizzle was a comfort.

When I left Gran's house that day, I walked around her yard and down by the fence until I found the bushes. The fence was a lopsided piece of old picket that Cranky had constructed decades earlier. I know that he had worked hours putting the fence around the perimeter of the backyard for the sole purpose of keeping *me* contained on my visits over to their house. Over the years, the slats had rotted and fallen into disrepair.

When I was eleven, Gran had me and Daddy take down most of it that summer, but since Cranky had built it himself, it brought tears to her eyes to watch what we were doing. In the end, she couldn't stand to see all of it go, and so she had requested for us to leave one section of it standing at the *bottom* of the yard where the lawn met the woods.

That was where the nandina bushes were. They were a sad sight. They looked like they were nothing more than several twigs sticking up from the ground. I don't know why, but I reached down and touched one of the leaves. It was smooth. It felt tender. I reached lower to where the stem forked off from the main branch and snapped the tender wood. The twig that I held in my hand was full of leaves and a few red berries. I put it in my pocket and made my way up the yard to my truck.

OVER THE COURSE of that spring there were two big things that happened in my life.

One, I started helping out at the greenhouses after school and on the weekends.

By then, I had been thinking about trying to get a job. I was finally old enough to join the work force. I was no longer considered a *minor*, and in the fall I would be going into my senior year of high school. Everybody was telling me that I needed a little experience under my belt before the real world set in, and I knew that they were right. It was time.

I bought a copy of *The Crow County Observer*, the area's only newspaper, and flipped to the back page where I began my search. Several blocks down, right below an ad for a full-time forklift operator, I saw it.

PART-TIME HELP NEEDED
Bush's Greenhouses is looking for a reliable person for afternoon and weekend work. Apply in person.

I went the very next day and applied. During the interview, Tom asked what I knew about watering, fertilizer, soil types, PH balance, nutrients, pest control, planting zones, shady and sunny locations, cold hardiness; the list went on and on. "Nothing sir," I told him, "but I am very eager to learn."

Tom looked at me, obviously confused about my presence, considering my lack of knowledge, and asked me if I had any experience *at all* working with plants. I was completely honest with him once again and told him that I didn't. I could tell that he was challenging my interest in the work by asking so many questions, but, in a way, I liked what he was doing. It made me feel like an adult.

I got the phone call from Tom two days later. To my surprise, he offered me the job, and I accepted right away. He must have seen something in me that I wasn't even aware of. I was to start the following Monday, right after I got out of school.

From there, I began to learn everything that I could about plants. I started my own garden at home. With a hoe and rake, and Momma's and Daddy's approval, of course, I tilled up a fifteen square foot block in the sunniest part of our back yard. After some research, I decided that I would start a night-garden.

That weekend, I constructed an arbor out of old timber that I found underneath the house. The arbor would serve as the entranceway into my garden. I planted a clematis vine that would hopefully trail up the posts. Inside the garden, I planted white peonies, woodruff, bleeding hearts, angels' trumpet, and of course, dusty miller. In a night-garden, at dusk and twilight, the white flowers and foliage stand out against the moonlight.

That first night, under the crescent moon, with the shovel still in my hand and Gravel sitting at my side, I stood in the center of the garden and looked around at my accomplishments. All the plants were small, and none of them had blooms, but I could only imagine what they would become with the proper patience and care. I had amended the dirt with black garden soil that added more contrast. That night, it was only the whitish foliage of the dusty miller that glowed under the moonlight.

Momma and Daddy came out of the house and stood there with me.

"Maybe this is the start of something new," Momma said.

"This might be a sign of what your future holds. With your new job and *this* under your belt, you might find out that you want to be a landscaper one day. You never know, all of this could develop into something," Daddy added. He was obviously impressed with what I had accomplished.

After they went inside, I stayed out there with Gravel. I looked at the sky that was full of shining stars and thought about the future. There was infinite possibility. Was Daddy right? Would I be a landscaper one day? Admittedly, all of this speculation about my possible career excited me about the prospect of working for the Bushes. But in the back of my mind, there was always the underlying reason that I had applied for the job in the first place—Nandina.

So, getting the job at the greenhouses was the first of the two most important things that happened to me that spring.

And the second, the one that was *the* most important, was that I got to know Nandina. It started out on the weekends with us spending time together, but by the time that she moved to Crow County at the end of May, I had already fallen in love.

6.

Bishopville, SC – the end of May...

THE PUNGENT SMELL of thick mud hung unwavering in the late spring night.

Nandina and Mala sat on the open tailgate of an old, abandoned pickup that had, at one time or another, been a bright, exciting shade of red. Over time, the paint job had become a rusty color of brown. It was a color that was not even close to the dark and soggy wetness of the surrounding swamp. Nandina sat there that night, staring into the black mud, and the thought occurred to her that the shade of rust really wasn't that far removed from the red dirt of her new home in Crow County. In a way, the color made her feel like she was finally ready for the move.

With her fingernail, she scraped at a flake of the rust until it popped free from the surface. It was her last night in Bishopville, and just as she had on so many other Friday nights over the past several years, she had gone to the swamp to hang out with her friends. For a long time, that particular spot of the swamp had been a special place for them.

The spot sat a good bit lower than the unlined, two-lane road that passed by the area of unmarred land. A short, narrow bridge with a dinged and scraped guardrail that was made of concrete and metal ran above the shallow water.

From the bridge, if you were standing there, you could see the truck that they sat on. It had been positioned next to the woods at a catawampus angle. To Nandina and her friends, it seemed like the front tires of the truck must have always been flat. It was hard for her to imagine them any other way. The rims were sunk so deep into the mud that the back end of the truck jutted upward, giving plenty of legroom between the tailgate and the earth.

Other than the two girls, the only other person that was present that night was a young man named Will Faulkner. Will was in front of the truck, sloshing around in the mud that came midway up the thick, rubber boots that he had worn just for the occasion. Each time that he would lift a foot, there was a noticeable suction sound as the rubber boot pulled free from the mud. The light from an oil lantern, that was just as rusty as the truck and sat on the tailgate next to Nandina, flickered over him, washing him in a soothing, orange glow. The lantern was the only light, save for the new moon and the scattering of stars that were overhead.

"Got him!" Will called out, breaking the quiet peacefulness of the night. In his right hand, he held up a squirming crawfish, showing it to the girls before tossing it into the plastic five-gallon bucket that was at his feet. The crawfish landed with a soft clatter against the others that Will had already caught that night.

"I'm going to miss all of this," Nandina quietly told Mala as she turned her attention away from Will and back to her friend. "You, Will, the swamp, catching crawfish, and..." Nandina swallowed the lump that was forming in her throat.

Mala placed her hand on Nandina's bent knee. "Nope," Mala said. "Don't you even think about it. You have a new life now. I'll be sure to visit you whenever I can, and you know you can come back here to see us. And besides, you've got Dusty now."

"Mala," Nandina said, cutting her off.

"I know, I know, you keep saying 'it's not like that' and all that other bull, but I can see right through it, Nanny."

"Mala, it's not," Nandina said again. "It's nothing like that. I've told you before, and I'll say it again, Dusty and I are just friends."

It was true. They were just friends. Over the past month, Nandina had been spending the weekends at the family's new house in Crow County and the rest of the school week with her uncle Colby who was right there in Bishopville.

For a month, she had been back and forth from one place to another. She felt like she was living two different lives—the one in Bishopville she loved wholly and knew that she would miss, but the one in Crow County was something new and it was full of possibility. For several weeks in May, it was as if she had been living in limbo—traveling between the past and the future.

She had gotten to know Dusty pretty well over the past several weeks. Aside from working together at the greenhouses, they would often spend time together—going for burgers or fishing at one of the local ponds. She could easily see a friendship forming between the two of them, but despite Mala's persistence and persuasion, she had zero interest in anything more.

"What have I already told you?" Mala spun her head around so that she was facing Nandina. The short, slim braids of Mala's hair twirled out, and the tiny sea shells that were woven into her hair softly clattered together like a gentle wind chime. "When I close my eyes, you know what I see?" Mala slammed her eyelids shut. "I see a triangle," she said and used each of her hands to draw the three-sided shape in the air. "This kind of triangle that I'm talking about has a girl and two boys." She opened her right eye and looked at Nandina in a lopsided squint. "It's a love triangle," she added, as if Nandina hadn't already caught on to what her friend was insinuating. "And you tell me, who doesn't enjoy one of those?"

"Unlike you, I don't have to have a boy in my life, Mala," Nandina insisted. "I can be happy on my own."

Mala laughed and dramatically slapped her own knee. "And this is coming from the girl that, on her first day at her new home, before she even got off the moving truck mind you, took a picture of Dusty while he was out running and minding his own business."

Mala was right. Taking the picture had been a silly thing to do. And then to show it to Mala had made it even worse. Nandina knew that Mala had a tendency to be overdramatic about everything. Mala had always been that way, even when they had been little girls and Mala would write those far-fetched love stories of princes and princesses. Knowing all of this, Nandina realized that in Mala's eyes, she and Dusty were probably already just one step from walking down the aisle.

Nandina turned bright when Mala brought up the photo. "Okay, okay" she relented. "You got me on that one, but..."

"It's not like you'd be doing anything wrong, Nanny. Jackson was the one that said he thought both of you should see other people while he was gone. So, do what he said and see other people."

Jackson. The real reason that Nandina wasn't ready to move on.

At the mention of Jackson's name, Nandina's memories spun her back in time to a night over a year earlier. Back then, Jackson had been part of the group. The foursome—Nandina, Mala, Will, and Jackson—had been close ever since the start of high school, and every Friday night they would meet up at the swamp. But Nandina had started feeling something else toward Jackson. She could tell that the feeling and attraction was reciprocated from him, but there seemed to be a constant grasping hand that was holding them back from falling headfirst over that cliff.

In an unusual set of circumstances that found Mala at home with a cold and Will being grounded for not doing his homework, Nandina and Jackson went to the swamp alone. The air was warm, sticky almost. In the distance, flashes of lightning portended a coming storm. Soon, cold drops of rain began to fall. In an effort to escape the rain, Nandina and Jackson jumped down from the tailgate where they had been talking and laughing. They could have easily trudged up the hill to the dry safety of his truck that was parked on the roadside near the bridge, but Nandina grabbed Jackson's hand and led him through the tall swamp grasses, around to the front of the rusty pickup. She opened the passenger side door, scooted across the vinyl seat, and patted the empty spot next to her, inviting Jackson to enter.

The interior of the truck smelled like the old, cheap air freshener that hung from the rearview mirror, swampy mud, and decades-old vinyl. Rainwater was dripping from both of them and pooling on the seat and the floor. After he sat down next to her, Jackson slammed the door shut.

By then, the rain was pouring down and pattering loudly on the truck's roof. With his hands, he rubbed his arms vigorously, saying "it's freezing." His teeth were chattering.

Nandina watched as Jackson reached into the glove compartment and pulled out a thick, squat candle. He reached into his front jeans pocket and pulled out a cigarette lighter. Jackson didn't smoke and Nandina later wondered if he had brought the lighter with him that night just for the purpose of lighting the candle.

The small, orange flame flickered around the cab of the truck. When their eyes met, whatever had been holding them back for so long finally let go. It was impossible to tell who leaned in to the other first because their lips met with such timely purpose and longing that it was as if everything in the world had been leading up to that particular moment.

But the kiss was only the beginning.

By the time that the rain had dropped to a soft drizzle, they were holding onto each other in a desperate need, like what they had just done was transcendental, and, really, it was. It had, in fact, changed everything.

Soon after, the rain picked up again but harder this time. Jackson was the one that broke the curtain of silence that was draped between them. "Did you know this was going to happen?" It was an impossibly innocent and boyish question that made Nandina smile. Both of their eyes were gazing through the rain-streaked windshield at the unrelenting storm.

Nandina's head was resting on Jackson's bare chest. She could feel his heart beating against her jaw. "What? The rain?"

Jackson laughed. "No, me and you. What we just did."

Nandina shook her head no. "Did you?"

"I might have helped, just a little bit, by pushing up the inevitable."

The inevitable. In Nandina's eyes, both then and now, that was exactly what everything with Jackson Archer had been, from the beginning to the end—inevitable.

Jackson's parents divorced when he was very young and his father moved away to North Carolina. Over the years, his dad had done very well for himself. He had started a successful farm-to-table restaurant, remarried over a decade earlier, and had two more children, a boy and a girl.

Everyone, including Nandina, knew that Jackson would one day move to North Carolina so that he could take over the family business, but no one expected it to be as soon as it turned out to be.

Just a year after that rainy night, the heart-wrenching news of Mr. Archer's failing health was spoken by Jackson for the first time.

"Cancer," Jackson had told Nandina with tears in his eyes. "They say he only has about a year to live."

The decision was quickly made. Jackson would move to North Carolina to be with his father during his last days while learning the ins and outs of the restaurant business so that, when the time finally did come, he would be ready.

"Why don't we put everything on hold?" The suggestion by Jackson had taken Nandina by surprise. "I mean, I love you, but we're still young. We should see other people and test the water a little bit. Just to make sure, you know?"

No. She didn't know. And even after two months had passed, she didn't think she would ever understand his reasoning. To her, the idea seemed cold and selfish.

"He'll be back in no time," Mala assured her. "Before you know it, he'll be crawling back into your arms."

Nandina glanced over her own shoulder and could see through the back glass of the truck that the candle was still on the dashboard where they had left it. On that rainy night with Jackson, the wick had burned for so long that most of the candle had melted down. Now, what remained of it was stuck in place by the hardened wax that had pooled around its base.

THE NEXT DAY, Nandina placed the last of the cardboard boxes on the floor of her new bedroom and took a good long look around. Other than the boxes, suitcases, and garbage bags that were full of clothes, the room was bare. Like the future, the white walls and polished hardwood floors were a blank slate that she could do anything with.

Finally, everything was done—all the moving, school, everything. Her junior year was over, and, for better or worse, she was officially out of Bishopville for good.

And as much as she tried not to, she missed it already.

She walked over to the large set of windows and pushed the sheer, white curtain aside. The sunlight was bright. She could feel the heat of the day through the glass.

After turning the latch that was at the top of the window, she pushed the bottom pane up. The air was hot and still, but it felt perfect. It smelled like turned earth and pollen. A bee buzzed around the open window right in front of Nandina, as if asking for permission to go inside before eventually flying off.

Her second story bedroom overlooked the greenhouses. There were several cars in the parking lot. She could hear a woman's laughter and the sound of tires crunching over the gravel of the driveway as one car was leaving.

Below her, Dusty emerged from the center greenhouse carrying what looked like a tray of dragon-wing begonias. After he placed the tray in the trunk of an old lady's car, he looked up at Nandina, smiled, and waved at her before going back to work inside the same greenhouse that he had come out of.

Nandina turned away from the window and felt overwhelmed by the monumental task of unpacking that was in front of her. No time like the present, she thought just before walking over to the closest box and peeling the flaps back.

Two hours later, after neatly placing her folded clothes in the dresser drawers and the hanging ones in the narrow closet, there was something across the room that caught her eye. It was underneath the old, boxy radiator that sat next to the door.

Was that pink and blue zebra-print?

She walked over to it, got down on her hands and knees, and reached underneath the radiator and pulled it free.

It was a shoebox that had a zebra-print folder lying flat on top. The folder was covered with a layer of dust and spider webs.

With the side of her bare hand, Nandina wiped the surface clean.

On the front of the folder, a name was written in girlish cursive—Kelly Brighton.

Nandina opened the folder. There were several sheets of ruled notebook paper that were tucked inside the right-hand flap. The pages were discolored with age. Nandina slid them out of the pocket. It appeared to be a story or school assignment that had been written in the same handwriting as Kelly Brighton's.

Sitting on the floor, Nandina began to read.

PERENNIALS – A HAUNTING LOVE STORY

It was the year of 1925 when the Blade family moved to Crow County from Chattanooga, Tennessee.

Nationwide prohibition had been in full swing for the past five years, but that didn't stop Mr.

Blade from distilling and selling his own liquor, both from his prior home in Tennessee and his new home.

Similar to the location in Tennessee, Thomas Blade's Crow County liquor stills were well hidden deep within the bramble of the woods behind the Blade family home.

The house had been built before the Civil War and had served as the home of Confederate soldier, Jasper Holt, among others.

Of course, selling illegal moonshine wasn't the Blades' only source of income. They owned and operated the saw-blade factory, Blade Manufacturing.

Both Mr. and Mrs. Blade relished their money and would often host lavish parties at their new home. According to one local man, who wishes to remain anonymous, "My parents went to one of those shin-digs," he said. "It was Halloween night. They said that everybody was wearing elaborate costumes and that the Blades had gone hog-wild with their extravagance. The whole house had been decorated with cardboard and crepe paper skeletons and witches. Lit jack-o-lanterns were everywhere. Mr. Blade's own moonshine poured like water. They even had a fortune teller that sat in the parlor room in front of a big crystal ball.

The fortune teller told Mrs. Blade that she felt a presence in the house."

Mr. and Mrs. Blade had two daughters, Fay and Hayley. They were twins. Both of the girls were beautiful like their mother, with long, dark hair and a pale complexion. And while each of the girls could have had any man that she wanted, Fay's choice in a suitor troubled Mr. Blade.

Ambrose Fletcher was eighteen years old. He had a strange purple mark that covered nearly the entire right side of his face. He lived with his family in their old farmhouse and worked at the greenhouses that were on the property. It was obvious that they, unlike the Blades, were scratching to get by.

Mr. Blade viewed the Fletchers as low-class and demanded that his daughter have nothing to do with Ambrose.

And so, defying her father's request because she was in love, Fay began to see Ambrose behind her father's back. Often, she would sneak out in the middle of the night to meet Ambrose in the center greenhouse. They vowed to one another that they would find a way to make the relationship work, despite her father's wishes.

Soon, Fay got sick and was not seen for seven months, not even by Ambrose. In fact, no one was let in the Blade household, out of fear of spreading the contagion.

On a day, when Fay had been home alone, the house was raided by three men who came in through the front door. Fay must have emerged from her upstairs bedroom to see what the commotion was about and caught the men off guard. When Mr. Blade came home, he not only discovered that the basement's inventory of moonshine had been emptied, but he found his daughter lying at the top of the stairs with multiple gunshot wounds. Her white nightgown was soaked through with blood.

The three men were caught with the car full of moonshine near Columbia. When questioned about the murder of Fay, they admitted to what they had done. They were each charged and got life sentences. It turned out that they were not smuggling the moonshine for profit. Instead, they were activists who supported prohibition, believing that alcohol was part of the devil's work and were doing what they thought was right by ridding the county of any and all libations.

When Ambrose Fletcher found out about what had happened to his beloved Fay, he was so devastated that he went into the perennial greenhouse where they had secretly met so many times in the past and took his own life.

Both families were so overtaken with grief with what had happened to their children that they packed up and fled from Crow County, never to return.

The Fletchers sold both their home and greenhouse business. Mr. Blade, on the other hand, chose to sell the factory but held on to the old home. Despite the fact that the property has remained in the Blade family ever since, the house hasn't been lived in since the tragedy. It remains a mystery as to who the sole proprietor is.

Over the years, people have speculated that the fortune teller from that Halloween party had predicted the death of Fay. People say that somehow the woman must have seen the murder before it ever happened.

It is Fay's ghost that people claim haunts Abandoned Manor. Sometimes at night, it is believed that Fay's spirit wanders from the home and to the greenhouse where she and Ambrose continue their love affair, even after death.

Nandina lowered the paper. Goose bumps were covering her arms.

She wondered if it was this house that Kelly Brighton had written about. Was the story based on fact, or was it some fanciful concoction that the Brighton girl had made up, similar to the fairy tales that Mala used to write about when they were kids and the romantic stories that she liked to focus on now?

She placed the notebook paper back into the interior pocket, closed the folder, and set it aside.

She lifted the lid on the shoebox.

Inside was an old, silver skeleton key that was resting on top of several photos.

Nandina lifted the key from the box. Looped through the end was a metal tag that had one word stamped into it—PERENNIALS.

She placed the key on the floor and picked up the photos. The first one was of a fancy house that Nandina immediately recognized as the antebellum-style home that she had seen that first day of arriving in Crow County. There was an embossed pink label that read—ABANDONED MANOR.

The second photo was of a pair of shabby-looking, wooden framed greenhouses that had morning glory vines growing up the sides and over the top. The vines were covered in purple flowers. The buildings appeared to be set within overgrown woods, so Nandina assumed that they were not the same ones that her family had recently purchased. This photo also had one of the pink labels attached—THE GREENHOUSES.

The third photo was what gave Nandina pause. It was very clearly a shot of the house that she was in. THE FLETCHER HOUSE.

The goose bumps that were on her arms spread all over her body. The hairs on the back of her neck stood on end.

Across the room, the curtains on the window moved. It was as if there had been a sudden, quick gust of wind or a long, deep intake of breath that had pulled them in.

Just as the curtains settled back down, there was a knock on the bedroom's open door that caused Nandina to jump. She spun around on her bottom to see Dusty standing in the doorway.

At the sight of him, she laughed out of relief and realized that it had only been the opening and closing of the downstairs door that had caused the draft that moved the curtain.

"You scared me half to death," she said.

.

7.

O N THE NIGHT of the first murder, it was a sheriff by the name of Richard Tomlin that the press was hammering with questions.

People wanted to know—Are there any leads? Do you believe that this is the work of a serial killer?

On TV, Tomlin, a middle-aged, balding man who looked battered and worn thin by the stress, stood in front of the news reporters and answered the questions to the best of his ability.

"Yes," he said. "Because of the ritualistic nature, and the way that the murder scene was arranged, we have reason to believe that this is a serial case. There are a few strong leads that we are looking into, but nothing concrete as of right now."

Even though the murder of Mary Gold had happened over a hundred miles from Crow County, seeing this on TV made me uneasy, reasonably so.

Due in a large part to movies and TV shows, everybody tends to have an idea of what they think a serial killer looks like, how one behaves in his day to day life, and what his mannerisms are. I know I did, but I'll spare you the descriptive details that I envisioned back then.

When I was little, I was always told not to associate with certain people; those that come from *the wrong side of the tracks* I would hear people say.

Hearing this, I did what almost any young boy would do—I let my imagination run wild. I created a place in my mind where the bad people came from. I called it *The Wrong Side*.

The area was littered with ramshackle houses that were nearly falling down. The sky was always dark with threatening storm clouds, yet no rain *ever* fell. The ground was so dry that, in places, it was cracked open as if hell itself were opening up.

Even though we lived in Crow County, there really wasn't an overabundance of crows in my day to day life, but within *The Wrong Side*, they were everywhere. The birds were perched on the dead tree limbs that reached out over the tainted ground and on the eaves of the low rooftops that were covered with damaged shingles.

Broken bicycles were on people's porches. Empty milk jugs and beer cans lay wherever they had been aimlessly tossed into the tall weeds. A dirty, plastic high-chair sat out of place next to a rusty mailbox at the end of a short driveway, giving the sad indication that someone had been unfortunate enough to have been raised in that terrible place.

In my younger, childish mind, it was those kinds of environments where killers and other bad people were born and bred.

I hadn't thought about *The Wrong Side* in months until a day when Tom, Rose, and I were unloading a trailer full of compost. This was right after I started working for them, and before the first murder.

I couldn't believe that they had taken the time to relocate *dirt* of all things, but Tom explained to me that the compost had been something that they had been working on for years.

"Good dirt is the key factor in growing things," Rose added. She was standing off to the side. Her white t-shirt was dirty from the work that we were doing. She had on one of those big, round straw hats. Like both me and Tom, she had on a pair of work gloves. Hers were too big and looked nearly ready to fall off her small hands. "It nurtures and gives the proper nutrients to the young seedlings, helping them grow into beautiful and prosperous adult plants."

Tom and I were standing on top of the compost pile. From where we stood, with shovels and pitchforks in hand, we scooped the dirt into the bins that had been placed next to the far right greenhouse, well out of sight from any customers that would park in front.

"Think of it this way," Tom said. He stood up straight and proudly. Sweat glistened on his forehead and lean arms. He shoved the pitchfork prongs into the thick compost next to his feet and removed the green trucker cap from his head. He wiped his forearm across his brow and then placed his hands on his hips. He was wearing an old pair of jeans and, like Rose, a white t-shirt. "You wouldn't want to raise a family in poor conditions; a dirty or broken home for example. Plants are the same way. They need a good foundation to grow. It all starts with good, quality dirt."

I'll admit that what they were saying did have a certain amount of weight to it. I thought about *The Wrong Side* and its easy black and white view of good and evil. To be honest with you, I missed that simple way of understanding, but by then, I knew that things were way more complicated than that.

Just within the past twelve months, I had seen firsthand that nice homes can sometimes be a façade to darkness.

ON JANUARY THIRD of the previous year, I went fishing with my best friend, Tyler Braxton, for the last time.

The day had been unseasonably warm. The high was near eighty. In just a few short days, school was going to resume after the Christmas break.

Tyler had been complaining about an abdominal pain off and on for days, but we thought nothing of it. We were sixteen! Unstoppable! We had laughed off the pain as a bad case of gas.

The trees around the pond were bare. Since the day was so warm, the leafless branches were one of the few signs to remind us of the season that we were in—January instead of April.

Countless blackbirds and red-breasted robins were flittering about the ground. If he'd still been living, Cranky would've said that it was a sign of a coming winter storm and that the birds were searching for seeds to store. I thought that they were just enjoying the warm weather.

I backed my truck up to the pond, so that we could fish from the tailgate. From the toolbox, underneath an old, rumpled t-shirt, I pulled out a half empty jar of moonshine that Bartley had given me several months earlier that had undoubtedly been swiped from his father's stash.

In addition to the moonshine, a bag of pork rinds from The Crow's Nest, a local BBQ shack, sat on the tailgate between us.

"Have you and Moira done it yet?" Tyler asked me.

Moira and I had been dating since the previous October.

"Sort of." I shrugged my shoulders and kept my attention on the cork in the water, waiting for it to bob under.

Tyler laughed. "What do you mean *sort of*? You either *have* or you *haven't*."

"We were going to, but...I guess you could say it was over before it ever got started." I could feel myself turning red at the admittance of my juvenile failure.

Chomping on the crunchy pork rinds, Tyler laughed so hard that it caused a flock of blackbirds from one of the nearby trees to erupt into flight.

Out of the corner of my eye, I saw him drop his fishing pole. His right hand went to the side of his face. He spit a bloody string of saliva onto the ground.

"Are you okay?" I asked him.

He nodded his head. "I just bit the inside of my cheek." He spit again. "But I'll be alright."

We caught a bucketful of bream by the end of the afternoon. The sight of the dropping sun was a sad overture to the otherwise perfect day. Just as the sky was the deepest blue before turning black, we made a pact. Best friends forever.

We loaded up the truck and headed home.

The abdominal pain that Tyler had been complaining about that day went away, but soon he was having a spiking fever that was causing him to have night sweats. He experienced a severe loss of appetite, headaches, and backaches. He was often confused about simple things like where he had left his boots or what should have been, to him anyway, easy math equations. That week, he failed an algebra test. It was the first test that he had *ever* failed. All of this was strange, but the strangest thing of all was when I called him the next weekend and asked him to go fishing and he turned down my invitation. I could tell over the phone that he had a shortness of breath.

Finally, he went to the doctor. It turned out that he had been born with a heart defect. The doctor told him that he had something called Infective Endocarditis, a condition where bacteria attaches itself to the outside of the heart, usually on an abnormality of the heart wall. Those with heart defects, or people that have had Rheumatic Fever, are far more likely to develop the infection. The doctor believed that the bacteria had entered Tyler's bloodstream through the wound that he had gotten from biting the inside of his cheek.

He was admitted to the hospital right away, but within days, the bacteria had spread.

They tried everything they could to help him, but despite their best efforts, it was too late, and Tyler succumbed to the illness.

Not long after Tyler's funeral, rumors and gossip began to fly around the area. People said that Tyler had been born with the heart defect because his mother, Jenny Braxton, drank and did drugs while she was pregnant with him. Some reacted so strongly to the accusations that one morning it was discovered that the word Murderer had been spray painted in red on the outside of the Braxton family home.

It didn't take long for Mrs. Braxton to withdraw from the rest of the community. On the rare occasion where she was spotted outside, it was said that she was so visibly emaciated that she was nothing but skin and bones. Her hair was so thin that, in spots, you could even see her scalp. And for this reason, she kept her head covered most of the time with either a hat or a hood. People said that what was happening to her body was because of methamphetamines and alcohol.

But the woman I knew as Tyler's mother wasn't like that, I reminded myself. I had known her my entire life, and I knew that she wouldn't have done something so foolish while she was carrying a baby.

The Jenny Braxton that I knew was a prim and proper woman. She was always dressed impeccably. She never left the house without makeup. Her blonde hair was cut and styled at the fancy beauty shop in town. She had a handsome, wealthy husband and a well-rounded son that everybody seemed to like. To me, she was a second mother.

When I was little and would go to their house for sleepovers and movie night, Jenny would go to bed way before the rest of us, claiming that eight hours of sleep just wasn't enough. *Beauty rest*, I remember her saying time and time again. *I need my beauty rest.*

From the floor of the living room, I would watch as Jenny made her way down the hall and disappeared through the blue door that led to her bedroom.

They lived in a very nice house that was not far from mine. In addition to being a well-regarded agent that specialized in farm insurance, Mr. Braxton owned and operated a pecan farm, and it was there, nestled within those neat rows of large trees, where the house stood. The Braxtons put a lot of work into their home. Next to Abandoned Manor and the Vance's, it was probably the nicest house in Crow County.

It was not the type of house that you would expect something like meth and alcohol abuse to dwell.

IT WAS A fittingly gloomy, rainy day in the spring after Tyler's death when I first heard about Jenny's past.

I was at Gran's house. Gran and Catherine were in the kitchen where they were making preserves out of the last of the figs that Catherine had picked from her own backyard tree.

I was in the den, sitting on the floor and watching TV. Gravel was lying next to me. He had his head resting on my bent knee, and in his slumber, the old dog would drool every now and then.

The den opened up into the kitchen, making it easy to see and hear what was going on from one room to the other. There were the sounds of boiling water and the clink of glass jars.

The entire house was filled with the smell of sugar and figs that, every so often, would cause Gravel to lift his head and sniff at the air. The aroma was undeniably what was making him drool in his sleep and led me to wonder what kind of sweet, nectarous dreams the fragrance was evoking.

I would occasionally break away from what I was watching to glance over at Gran and Catherine. They were each wearing loose fitting dresses that had flowers printed all over them. Muumuus, I think they are called. A white apron was tied around each of their necks and hips. Catherine's blue hair was styled in tight curls while Gran's white hair nearly brushed her shoulders. They talked and giggled as they worked. They, along with Gravel asleep and drooling on my leg, made me smile.

When the subject of Tyler got brought up, Catherine was quick to say, "You know what they're saying is right. When that boy's momma was a girl, she had a wild streak in her as big as my behind. She would party everyday from sun up 'til sun down if she could. It's a real shame, if you ask me."

According to Catherine, Jenny was the only child of a single mother named Vivian. They had lived in the center of three houses at the end of Saw-Blade Road.

During Jenny's teenage years, the young girl showed every sign of falling under the easy spell of entrapment that the place of Saw-Blade Road offered in such wild and salacious abundance. It was in the way that she dressed and talked. Even if you didn't know her, you could guess where she was from just by the way that she swung her hips in her little cut off jean shorts that let the bottom of her butt-cheeks show. She hung out with the wrong crowd and chose a quick rendezvous with the bad boys over a long-term relationship every time. It was gin that she guzzled like water.

"Gin-Jen is what they called her," Catherine said.

But somehow, Gin-Jen managed to escape. While she was a senior in high school, it appeared that she began to turn things around. She started dating a boy from a well-to-do family, Ryan Braxton.

Soon, they were married, and they lived in a small house that stood amid the evenly spaced rows of pecan trees that would soon begin to turn a meager profit for the family. It wasn't much better than the houses from where she had grown up, but it was a step in the right direction. It was not Saw-Blade Road.

Within two years, they added on to the small house, turning it into the nice, ranch-style home that I had always known. It was where they had raised Tyler.

One time, not long after Tyler died, I went to the Braxton house by myself. I was going to offer my condolences, which I had failed to do up until that point, largely in part because of everything that I had been hearing about Jenny. I, like almost everyone else, placed a certain amount of blame on her for what had happened to Tyler.

The small, red buds on the pecan trees were bursting open with new, green leaves. On the outside wall of the house, someone had tried to clean the spray painted word off the brick, but had left a messy looking smear of crimson.

Normally, I would have gone to the door underneath the carport, the one that led into the kitchen, and just opened it like I lived there, but that day I went to the front door instead. Thinking back on it now, subconsciously I felt like I no longer belonged there.

I knocked on the door and Ryan, Tyler's dad, answered. He was wearing a pair of jeans and a tucked-in, blue polo shirt. He had dark bags under his eyes. I could tell that he hadn't been getting much sleep. It was the first time that I had seen him since the funeral.

Out of courtesy, I removed the cap from my head.

I nodded my head toward him. It was a silent, manly *I hope everything's okay* kind of nod. "I just wanted to come by and say how sorry I am about everything that happened. I know I should've come by sooner but..."

Ryan shook his head. I knew that it was a gesture indicating that there was no need for me to continue. "Come in," he said and led me into the house.

I was nervous about seeing Jenny. Would she really look like what people had described? Would she resemble one of those meth addicts that you see on TV? But I didn't see her anywhere. I didn't even hear her moving about.

Instead, what I saw inside was shocking. Near the door were countless boxes, marked on the outside with black marker—KITCHEN, BATH, CLOTHES, BOOKS, PICTURES, OFFICE.

It was the last two boxes that had caused my eyes to dart across the living room.

The office was empty. The walls and floor were completely bare. There wasn't even a picture left hanging on the wall. There was no chair, desk, pen, notebook or anything.

I looked back at him. I must have looked stunned because he quickly offered up an explanation.

"We're getting divorced," he said.

Those three words summed up everything that I was seeing.

I sat down in a chair that was pushed up against the wall in the living room.

"Do you know what she does in there?" He nodded toward the closed, blue door at the end of the hallway that led into their bedroom. Tears were welling up in his eyes. I had never seen him cry.

So that was where Jenny was. She was in the bedroom.

"Sometimes she drinks so much until she blacks out," he said. He walked over to the coffee table and picked up a large sheet of thin paper. When he tuned around to face me, I knew that what I was seeing was the blueprint to some type of building. He held up the large sheet of paper so that the floor plan was facing me. In what was about the center of the blocky diagram, something had been repeatedly circled, over and over again, in red ink. "You see this?" His finger was at the epicenter of that manic vortex. "This is where she is right now."

The visual aid showed me the room where Ryan claimed that she was, but why? And who had marked it in red? And what did it matter anyway? What was so special about that room?

He began to fold the paper until all that was visible was the area that had been circled—their bedroom.

"Look," he said and held the floor plan closer to me. "Don't you see it? Our bedroom *is* the original house. We built everything else, all of this," he motioned with his arms at our surroundings, "around the original house that we lived in when we first got married."

I could see that the sketch of the room that he was showing me, when looked at by itself, was in fact big enough to be a house on its own.

One time, a long time before that day, I had gone into the Braxton's bedroom with Tyler.

I remember thinking how strange all of it was. There was a brick wall surrounding the outside of the bedroom door. When the door opened, there was a short hallway on the other side that led into a sitting area that was complete with a couch and

TV, unlike any other bedroom I had ever seen. In addition to a small corner closet that was next to the bed, there was an enormous walk-in off the right, which must have been the original kitchen, I reasoned, based on what Ryan was showing me on the blueprint.

"And now," Ryan continued, "it's almost like she wants to be back there, in that tiny one bedroom house that we used to have. It's like something is pulling her into the past and there is nothing that I can do to stop it."

Is that what all of this was about? Was she having a relapse and going back to her old ways? Now, with Tyler gone, maybe she was looking for an escape, and she chose to do it the only way she knew how—with drugs and alcohol.

There was a sound of a clicking lock. It was a heavy, ominous sound that broke my train of thought.

Both Ryan and I turned to look.

At the end of the hallway, the blue door eased open just a crack. I could tell that it was dark on the other side.

Then there was a voice. It was a weak, raspy female moan that came from the other side of the door. "Get out," the voice slurred.

I looked at Ryan. I had seen my fair share of possession movies and that was exactly what the voice brought to mind. I felt goose bumps cover my arms.

I thought about that word that had been spray-painted on the outside of their house—*murderer*. For some reason, a memory from a Halloween night in which Jenny had been wearing a black witch hat flashed through my mind.

"Get out!" She screamed it this time.

I wondered, was the word directed at both of us or just me?

"I um, I'm going to head out," I said to Ryan and started making my way to the front door.

As I was about to open the door, Ryan spoke up behind me. "Dusty," he said.

I turned around to face him. He was reaching into his front jeans pocket.

"We wanted you to have this." He held out his hand. A silver necklace dangled from his fingers. On the end was a silver cross. I knew that it had belonged to Tyler. When he had been alive, the necklace had hung from the rearview mirror of his truck.

I took the necklace from him. "Thanks," I said and glanced down the hallway one more time at the blue door.

I left their house that day with my mind working overtime.

Was it true? Had Jenny relapsed into Gin-Jen all over again? Was it grief over Tyler that had caused her to go deep into the past?

That night, when I tried to sleep, I had a nightmare.

I was walking down a long hallway that had a blue door at the end. Just before I reached it, the door swung open on its own. On the other side was what looked like a world that had been created of dark fantasy. The sky was black with storm clouds. The ground was parched and cracked. Every tree limb was bare. A murder of crows flew past. It was *The Wrong Side*.

Then, through the grim landscape, there was a woman approaching. Her body was emaciated. Underneath a cheap, dollar store witch hat was thin, blonde strands of damaged hair. She was wearing a black halter top, jean shorts, and rubber flip-flops that were neon pink.

When she smiled, I saw that both her top and bottom rows of teeth were rotted.

She held her arms up toward me, as if offering an embrace.

I woke up before letting her wrap her arms around me, but I wondered if the dream was telling me that it was time to step away from my childish views of good and evil and let the truth envelop me. It was time to grow up. In the real world, things are not always black and white, as I had once imagined. Things are way more complicated than that. And sometimes, malevolence exists exactly where you would least expect it.

8.

DADDY AND I rode in complete silence all the way home from the hospital. The radio was on, but it was turned down so low that it was barely audible against the steady hum of the truck's large tires as they moved along the highway. I tried to listen to the lyrics of the music, but my mind just wasn't in the right place. Instead, it was back there at the hospital with Rose and Nan. I was scared for both of them.

After we had finally gotten out of the city, the sky was dark overhead. As I sat in the passenger seat, I remember looking up through the windshield of my truck. It was a relief to finally be able to see the stars shining so brightly again.

The way that the sky looks out in the country is another thing that makes me know that I don't want to live in a big city. Just being in the city at dusk is sad. You feel cocooned, like everything is pressing in on you. Even when you're outside, you don't get that wide open feeling that you do when you're out in the sticks. Nighttime in the city is almost like there is something that is separating you from the rest of the sky.

When I was little, it was decided by scientists that Pluto was no longer a planet. Sometimes, when I look at the night sky, I think about the presence of what was once known as Pluto. It's kind of like losing someone, I think. My analogy is like this—Pluto *was* a planet and Tyler *was* my best friend, and even though he is physically gone, I know that he, like Pluto, is still out there somewhere. Do you see what I mean?

We stopped at our house so that I could get a few things that I would need for my time at The Vance's. Momma pulled in right behind us.

When I opened the door, I saw that Gravel was already there waiting on the other side. He immediately hobbled down the steps, hiked his leg, and peed on the dead plant from two Christmases ago. It struck me in a strange way that I would miss that plant if it wasn't there.

While I waited on Gravel to finish doing his business, I looked across the yard to my garden. There were a few white flowers and the foliage of the dusty miller that appeared lustrous in the moonlight.

Daddy went into the house, flipping on every light in the process.

Momma stood on the tiny porch with me. Her arms were crossed. I could tell that she was surveying the woods that stood across from us. Even though neither of us said it, I knew that she was on the lookout for the killer.

I tried not to be paranoid, but I was.

Gravel wobbled back up the steps. I let him walk into the house ahead of me.

When we were back inside, Momma shut the door and flipped the deadbolt. Even though I had heard the sound of the lock clicking into place countless times over the years, for some reason that night it was extra loud. It was a proclamation against danger.

You can't get us! You won't!

"We're going to the store tomorrow to get a new door and locks," she said.

The door had been part of our house for as long as I could remember. It was one of those doors that had a small glass window at eye level. It's the kind that you could imagine a man shattering the glass with his fist then reaching his arm through and simply unlocking the door.

Daddy spoke up from the other room. "Did they call back about the alarm system?"

"They said that they won't be here until Monday morning. The number's on the refrigerator," she answered.

By then, I was already in my room and I could hear the rest of their conversation through the house. Daddy was going to use some of his sick-time so that he could be there for the service people on Monday morning.

I was never a messy teenager. I kept my room clean and well organized so that I knew where everything was. There was never dirty underwear or socks thrown onto the floor. All of my clothes were either folded or hung and put away. The only things on my nightstand were an alarm clock and a lamp. I made my bed every morning. The top of my dresser wasn't cluttered—there was only a small, silver tray that I kept my watch, wallet, and pocket change in, and a framed photo that stood on the right-hand side.

The photo was an old black and white that had been discolored with age. The top corner held a stain of some kind. The bottom edge was creased, and all four sides were worn. The subject of the photo was Gran and Catherine when they had been around my age. They were at the end-of-the-school-year summer bonfire that had been a J.H. Academy tradition, even back then.

I opened the closet and grabbed a duffle bag that I threw some clothes into, not really paying attention to what I put in there. Gravel watched what I was doing, and I could tell that he knew that I was going somewhere. He sat on the floor and watched me with a sad look in his eyes, pleading for me not to go. It always tore me up when he did things like that.

There was a small bathroom located off my bedroom. I went in there and got the toiletries that I would need for the next several days.

After telling Gravel goodbye and giving him a doggie treat out of the jar in the kitchen, both of my parents walked with me to the truck.

Daddy drove again. I sat in the passenger seat, and Momma was in the middle between us.

The Vance property was only a few miles from where we lived. In fact, when we were kids, Bartley and I would walk through the woods to our houses. Back then, there had been a footpath where we traveled. I wondered if it was still there.

First off, one of the main differences between the Vance house and ours is the location. Whereas ours is set back in the woods, off that small, red dirt road, and the Vance family lived in a two-story mansion that sits on top of a grassy, neatly mowed hill. The home is easy to spot from the main highway. All of the land that surrounds it is theirs.

Bartley's dad had been born into money and had made a lot more hustling real-estate through his own company.

When we pulled up to the Vance house that night, Daddy had to press the button on the intercom that was next to the tall gate. The speaker crackled to life.

It was only a brief moment before there was a voice that came through. "Come on in, Thomas." It was Mr. Vance, Bartley's dad, speaking to us from somewhere inside the home. It was obvious that he was viewing us through one of the cameras that they had positioned all throughout the interior and exterior of the house.

In front of us, the gate began to open. It was a slow and dramatic process, like something you'd see in a movie or TV show.

My dad made a small guffaw as he stared straight ahead at the moving gate. He seemed mesmerized by it. "Money," he said and shook his head with disbelief. "They've got it. Plenty," he added for emphasis.

After the passageway was wide enough, we drove through. I looked over my shoulder and saw that the gate was already closing behind the tail end of my truck.

The inclining driveway was smooth under the truck tires. It was solid, black tar. As we approached, the Vance house stood like a fortress in front of us.

The house had been constructed with solid red brick. It seemed that every light was turned on. Climbing jessamine vines grew up the wall on each side of the door and were lit with a pair of spotlights that shined up from the ground. A wide set of steps led up to the small, circular brick porch. An enormous light fixture hung above the front door. To the right of the house was a curvy, brick wall that wrapped around the swimming pool. Like the walls of the house, this one had jessamine growing on it and was lit in the same way. From where we sat in the driveway, I could see the water reflecting and shimmering against the palmetto trees that stood on the other side of that wall around the pool.

When I opened my door, I could smell the chlorine.

My father looked at me. "They'll catch whoever did this, Dusty."

I knew that he was talking about what had happened to Rose. I nodded my head. People kept saying things like that.

I shut the door and walked up the steps of the porch. My parents stayed in the truck and watched me to make sure that I made it inside safely. It kind of made me feel like a kid, but, at the same time, it comforted me.

Just as I was about to knock on the door, I heard my name being called from the other side of the brick wall that wrapped around the pool.

"Dusty, I'm 'round here." It was Mr. Vance.

I looked at my dad and waved, sending him off.

I noticed that the metal gate to the pool area was standing open.

When I walked in, I saw Mr. Vance sitting in a nice lawn chair at the far end of the pool. A low table sat next to him. He was placing a short drinking glass down, and it clinked when it made contact with the tabletop. The ice inside the glass rattled. I knew that it was whiskey he was drinking. It was his favorite. Around the pool were tables that had foldout chairs laying flat on top of them. Unplugged string lights were draped throughout the trees and some were pulled up into the center where they hung high, kind of making the shape of a circus tent. A black and white HAPPY BIRTHDAY banner was draped across the brick wall. It appeared that everything was ready for a birthday bash. I wondered briefly if the party had been cancelled because of the day's hellacious events.

"How's she doing?" Mr. Vance asked from his darkened corner. I knew that he was talking about Rose.

"Nothing's changed since this morning," I told him, and the words felt hollow coming from my lips.

I stepped closer to him and sat on the edge of the chair next to his. The table and whiskey separated us.

"That's too bad," he said, staring off into the water of the pool. "Well, look here. Bartley's not in yet. He went out with his friends. You can go ahead and sit your stuff in his room if you want. Pam's in the house somewhere."

I stood and walked across the width of the pool. By the time that I reached the sliding glass door that led into the house, Mr. Vance spoke again.

"You'll be safe here," he said.

I nodded in agreement and went inside.

Mrs. Vance, Pam, came rushing toward me from the kitchen. She was wearing a long, flowing white housecoat.

"Dusty!" she sounded happy that I was there. "I'm so, so, *so* sorry about what happened. I know that girl means a lot to you." I knew that she was talking about Nan.

"Yeah," I said. "I love her."

"I know you do, honey." The way she said it made it sound like it was an unfortunate thing, like she was sorry that I was in love with Nan. She looked around the room for a moment as if she was searching for what to say or do next, like it would just appear to her out of the blue. "Here, have a cookie," she said and lifted a silver serving dish of cookies from the coffee table. I hadn't even noticed the cookie tray before she made the offer.

"No thanks. I'm not hungry."

"Oh, you have to eat. I hope you've been eating since all of this happened." She placed the cookies back on the coffee table. "They'll be right here if you change your mind, sweetie." She looked at me and noticed the duffel bag that was strapped over my shoulder. "Oh. Oh, my goodness." She held her long, feminine fingers to her chest. "I am *so* sorry. I know you must want to put that heavy bag down. Bartley's room is down the hall to the right."

I actually laughed out loud then. I'll admit that it had been a long time since I had been in their house, but not *that* long. "I know where his room is," I told her and began to make my way toward the large, curved staircase that led to the second story.

"Of course you do! Of course you do," she said. "I'm just frazzled and all. I don't even know *what* I'm saying."

I turned around and looked at her. "Thank you...for letting me stay here," I told her from the middle of the stairs.

"Oh Dusty, you know that you're welcome to stay at our house whenever you want. Any time. *Any time*," she dramatically stretched out the words.

She was too much.

I continued to climb the stairs and knew that Mrs. Vance was still standing at the bottom, watching me. I could feel her eyes on my back, and I had to force myself not to turn around and glance at her.

The upstairs hallway, like several other rooms in the house, all four bathrooms, and the kitchen, had sensors next to the doorways so that when someone walked through, it would trigger a light to come on. The light that came on in the hallway was a small nightlight that was situated near the floor. It took me by surprise.

It had been nearly a year since I had been inside Bartley's room. I walked in, flipped on the light, and stood in the center of the room. The room was huge. It was bigger than the living room at our house. I thought it was funny how in a house that big, and with an extra bedroom, that I was expected to sleep in the same room as Bartley. I was seventeen, and he was eighteen. We were too old for sleepovers.

In addition to his bed, there was an old, green couch that was pushed up against the opposite wall. It was where I had always slept when we were younger. The couch had a blanket and sheets on top. A nice, brown leather recliner sat in the opposite corner. The same heavy dresser and nightstand from when we were kids stood on the floor. Instead of the posters of 4x4's that had once been thumbtacked to the wall, there were now several pictures of old houses that had been placed into nice, glass fronted frames. There were no teenage things cluttering up the floor or dresser. Instead, the polished antique dresser-top was the home to a neat stack of realty magazines that were held down by an old crystal doorknob. There was a framed photo of him and Moira.

I sat down on the edge of the chair in the corner. I texted Nan just to let her know that I had gotten to Bartley's house safe and sound. She texted me back just a minute later.

Good. Have a great night!

It was only a little after ten o'clock, but I was exhausted. The stress of the past couple of days had drained me.

I threw my duffel bag into the corner, and after showering in the large bathroom that was located just down the hall, I went to lie down on the couch.

I pulled the layers of blankets back and crawled underneath. Then I pulled the sheet up to my chin. It smelled clean, but at the same time, it smelled the way that clothes do when they have been crammed in the bottom of a drawer for months or even years. I imagined Mrs. Vance, earlier that night, pulling the sheets out of the closet and washing them upon learning that I would be staying at their house.

I tossed and turned for what seemed like forever. Moonlight crept through the slats of the window blinds and cast moving shadows of tree limbs on the floor. I had left the door slightly cracked, and there was the light from the hallway that shone through, creating an upright rectangle around the perimeter. The light stayed that way until its timer went out, plunging the hall into darkness. I couldn't help but imagine the door as being painted blue like the one at Gin-Jen's house. You know—the one that I often had nightmares about. I let this idea bother me so much that I had to eventually turn away from the door so that I was facing the back of the couch.

Despite being as tired as I was, sleep wouldn't come easily to me that night. Every time I closed my eyes, I pictured either Rose lying in the hospital bed or a dark figure standing outside of the Vance property, staring at the window to the room where I was trying to sleep. Being in a house that wasn't my own didn't help matters either. There were sounds that I wasn't used to hearing, and being as tense as I was, they were sounds of danger. Everything I heard could've been the killer lurking about through the large house.

Every time that I dozed off, there would be something that pulled me out of sleep a moment later, and I would wake, afraid. It was the kind of fear that I hadn't felt in a very long time.

For as long as I could remember, there had been a story of an old man that walked the roads of Crow County. A bag man, we called him.

Legend has it that he could be spotted at all times of the day and night, walking all alone up and down the road whistling a tune. He had a large, burlap bag that was flung over his shoulder.

Of course, I had never seen the man firsthand, but, when I was little, I had pictured him as being old and rail-thin. I thought that he probably wore overalls. When Gran used to tell me the story, I *knew* that he put little kids like me in the bag and walked away with them.

People said that the bag man lived inside of the old saw-blade factory. Because of the story, no one, and I mean *no one*, not even the bravest kids like Scoot Henderson, would dare go any where near the building, not even to tell stories or throw rocks at the windows.

One time, when I was around five or six years old, a tornado came through Crow County. To this day, I can still remember how the air had felt that mid-June morning. Everything was calm and eerily still. It was *hot.* I remember how early in the day there had barely been *any* dark clouds in the sky, but even without the ominous cloud cover, something felt off. It's hard to explain, but it just didn't feel *right* outside.

I remember that when I opened the door that morning, it was like I just knew that something bad was going to happen. Even Gravel, who had been just a puppy back then, had walked around the house with his tail tucked between his legs and his ears pulled back. Outside, because of the higher winds in the sky, all of the birds were flying low to the ground, another thing that the old people around the area said was a sign that a storm was approaching.

That morning, I had been dropped off at Gran and Cranky's house. Back then, in the summer months, I stayed with them during the day while Momma and Daddy were working. I usually took Gravel with me. I remember when I walked into the house on that particular morning, I was greeted with the usual smell of bacon and homemade biscuits, but that day there was also the sound of the TV. Hearing the TV in their house was such an anomaly that, it alone, set off my *something must be wrong* radar.

The weatherman was on the screen giving the ominous forecast for the rest of the day. *Tornado watch*, he said. I remember sitting on the floor, pretending to play with blocks, but listening to Gran and Cranky as they discussed the difference between a *watch* and a *warning*. I took it all in.

"A watch means that the conditions are *likely*," Cranky explained. "A warning—well, that means that a tornado has actually been spotted."

I can clearly remember playing with Gravel on the floor of the den. The TV stayed on all morning long. Every time that the alert would scroll across the TV, Gran would drop what she was doing and come into the den.

Please don't be a warning, I thought each time that the harsh sounding weather alert would start, and, most of the time, I was relieved to see that it was only a watch, but one time, just one, my fear came true.

TORNADO WARNING FOR THE FOLLOWING COUNTIES IN SOUTH CAROLINA – CROW – SEEK SHELTER IMMEDIATELY

Gran had been in the middle of fixing lunch. She was holding one of her large mixing bowls and a bright blue dish rag that she had been using to dry the bowl with. Cranky was sitting in his chair. There was a brief moment where all three of us were completely still, unsure what to do next, and then, I can so clearly remember this to this day, there was the sound of Cranky letting the footrest down on his recliner. It was a squeaky, grating noise.

Gran sat the bowl on an end table. Under normal circumstances, she would *never* do something like that. Everything in their house had a place, and I knew, even back then, that the end table was not the place for the bowl. For her to sit something somewhere that it didn't belong was just as good of a sign as the birds flying low that indicated that the situation was serious.

"Grab the dog," Cranky said as he was stepping into his boots.

I picked up Gravel and the four of us ran outside. By then, the sky had turned nearly black. The limbs on the pecan and oak trees were bent at unbelievable angles. Leaves and dirt were whipping across the yard. I could hear the heavy rain in the distance.

We went into the basement. It was the one and only time that I had ever been down there. Gran and Cranky had always told me *not* to go in the basement. They said that it was dangerous, *there could be snakes down there,* or *you could get hurt,* yet there we were. It smelled damp. There was a tall shelving unit along the farthest wall that was stacked full of canned vegetables and preserves, but, other than that, the space was empty. I remember being crouched on the dirt floor, holding Gravel tight to my chest, and hearing the blusterous wind outside. By then, the rain had reached us and was coming down in sheets. Tree branches scratched at the house, and there was the occasional loud crack of one of them snapping. I thought that it sounded like gunshots.

When the bare, hanging bulb that was overhead flickered and then went out completely, I assumed the worst. We stayed that way for a long time, huddled close together, until there was only the sound of calm on the other side of the wall. When we finally emerged from the basement, I was expecting to see destruction, but everything was relatively fine. It looked like a routine thunderstorm had passed through. Other than the small twigs that were scattered across the drenched ground, nothing seemed to be messed up. The sun was beginning to peak through the clouds and glistened on all the wetness. There was the sound of a chirping bird in the distance.

By the time that we got back inside the house, the phone was ringing. Gran answered. It was Momma. She was calling from work to make sure that we were all okay. She told Gran that she had heard from a coworker, who had heard from someone else, that the saw-blade factory had been destroyed in the storm.

I remember almost immediately thinking about the bag man. Like I said before, I had always been told that he lived in the factory building. I remember thinking, if his home has been destroyed, where will he go next? I imagined him walking away from the destruction with his big, burlap bag thrown over his hunched back and wandering the back-roads, whistling.

Up until then, I had always felt safe where I lived. I thought that as long as I stayed away from Saw-Blade Road and the old factory building I wouldn't be in any kind of danger, that everything would be okay, but after the day of the storm, I felt like everything had changed.

That night at the Vance's, all those years later, I was thinking about all of this as I tried to fall asleep. Everything slipped out of my waking consciousness and into the realm of dreams with ease once sleep finally came.

During an all too familiar dream, just as the blue door at the end of Gin-Jen's hallway swung open, I was jolted awake.

Something, somewhere, had woken me up. At first I was disoriented and confused about where I was. The sheet was tangled around my legs, making me realize that I must've been kicking and thrashing about in my fitful slumber. I was certain that the blue door hitting the wall had woken me up, but that had been in a dream, hadn't it? If it had been, I wondered, what was the earthly sound that had snapped me out of the dream?

It took me a moment, but I remembered that I was at the Vance's house. Realizing this, I turned over on to my other side and saw that the door to Bartley's room was open. A figure stood in the doorway, silhouetted by the low light coming from the hallway.

The dreams that I had been having still lingered on the edge of reality. What I saw in front of me was, all at once, several different beings. Remember that I had just woken up, and my imagination was running wild, but I clearly saw all of this. The hunched over bag man pointed his long, crooked finger at me, Gin-Jen, with her streaks of dirty blonde hair, cheap witch hat, and blood-shot eyes, held her arms up toward me, as if inviting me into an embrace, and finally, the Plant Killer was there, faceless and dark. The three of them were morphing and changing from one to the other like some cheap effect in an old horror flick.

I was in a panic by the time the figure took a jerky step forward. The moonlight from the window on the opposite side of the room washed over its features. It was Bartley.

As he walked into the room, I could tell that he thought I was sleeping.

He was trying to be as quiet as possible as he moved into the room and sat in the large chair in the corner where he promptly began to unlace his boots.

I wondered if he even knew I was there. I thought about making a noise like a small cough or simply rolling over just to let him know, but surely his parents had told him, hadn't they?

When he stood, he looked right in my face and leaned in close. He must've seen the moonlight sparkle across my open eyes.

He laughed. "Hey buddy, I didn't know you were awake," he said quietly. "Sorry to hear about Mrs. Bush." He took off his shirt and tossed it onto the chair. "Moira said to tell you that she was sorry too. She said to send you and Nan her best wishes."

I nodded my head and wondered when he had talked to Moira. To be honest, since they had broken up and she was away at college, I was surprised that they still talked at all.

9.

three months earlier...

FORGET THE SUMMER solstice. When you're seventeen, summer begins the moment the bell rings on the last day of school.

That year, it was a Friday, and the students of J.H. Academy only had to endure a half day of school.

Even though the sound of the bell was something that they heard all the time, it was this particular ring that they had been looking forward to the most.

It only took a split second for the classroom doors to swing open and the central hallway to fill with teenage excitement. Plans for the next three months echoed off the walls. There were the sounds of shuffling papers and books being shoved deep into worn-out backpacks where they would not be seen again until the end of August. Amid all the talk and laughter, you could hear words like *lake*, *beach*, and *party*. There was another pair of words that floated across the hallway like a ghost, entering ears and tantalizing thoughts—*bonfire* and *tonight*. The two words placed together had the power to change anybody's plans and cause even the most socially awkward juniors and seniors to imagine being there amongst the partiers.

Outside, even though it was not yet June, the weather was already nearly summertime hot. The sky was clear. White clouds hung like cotton across the wide expanse of blue. Some of the more adventurous girls of the school had worn their swimsuit tops underneath their school clothes and were now peeling off their tees and blouses in the parking lot. They piled into trucks and cars that spun out of the gravel parking lot on their way to freedom.

EVERY YEAR, SINCE 1925, the summer bonfire had been held in an old peach orchard that was located on the edge of the county line.

Over the past century, the orchard had been replanted several times, but the branches and trunks of the current trees were so gnarled and gray that they looked more like small live oaks.

Mala, who was always up for a party, was staying at Nandina's house that weekend. She had kind of invited herself, but Nandina couldn't imagine going to her first party of the summer without her best friend by her side.

They spent the afternoon just hanging out around the house. Mala helped Nandina finish unpacking the boxes that had been sitting in her room for too long. They hung up the framed reproductions of vintage seed catalogues that Nandina had been collecting over the past year. The whole time that they worked, they listened to new records on an old gramophone record player that had belonged to Nandina's grandmother, Lily.

Mala told Nandina that she had finally had a revelation about the romance novella that she was working on.

"I don't want to give away too much," she said, "but it's based on an old, Native American legend."

The topic of Mala's starry-eyed writing style made Nandina think about Fay's ghost wandering from Abandoned Manor to the old greenhouses searching for Ambrose.

Nandina showed Mala the handwritten ghost story. "When you're done, look in the box." She placed the old shoebox on the bed.

"Ooh, 'A Haunting Love Story'," Mala read from the story's title after she had the pages in her hands.

As Nandina showered, Mala sat on the floor with her back leaning against the bed and read the tale with wide-open eyes.

As soon as she found it, Nandina knew that Mala would like the romanticized story. With the doomed lovers, who continue to see each other even after death, it was Mala through and through.

In a way, Nandina envied Mala's fanciful view of the world in which true love always finds its way, no matter the circumstances. It was a girlhood confidence that Mala had clung to, and Nandina wished that she too was still able to see things that way.

But it was an ability that she had lost.

When Nandina came out of the bathroom with a towel wrapped around her wet hair, Mala looked up at her from her spot on the floor. She had tears in her eyes. The open shoebox was in her lap. She was holding the old skeleton key with her right hand.

"I absolutely love that you found this stuff. It's beautiful. I've read it three times."

Nandina had read the story herself and thought it was more spooky than beautiful, but to each her own, she thought.

"Let's go out there tonight," Mala suggested.

When it came time to get dressed, Nandina decided on a simple, v-neck gray tee, while Mala opted for a 1970's inspired, loose fitting brown frock that was printed with yellow dandelions. They fumbled around each other in the bathroom as they scrambled to get their makeup done before it was time for Dusty to pick them up.

Dusty pulled into the driveway right on time and met them at the front door. He was freshly showered after his late afternoon run. He was wearing his favorite t-shirt. The shirt was dark blue with the state emblem of a palmetto tree and crescent moon printed on the back.

On the way to the bonfire, Nandina sat between Dusty and Mala. Directly in front of her, a silver necklace with a cross on the end hung from the rearview mirror and would swing like a pendulum whenever the truck made turns or hit ruts in the old paved road.

When they got to the orchard, there was already a line of cars and trucks on the roadside, so Dusty had to settle for parking a good ways back.

From there, to get to the bonfire, they had to walk through the rows of aged trees, where everywhere that Nandina looked was a bounty of ripe peaches waiting to be picked by the field workers.

As they moved through the orchard, every so often Nandina would catch a glimpse of the orange embers from the fire as they floated high above the peach trees and into the night sky where they seemed to disappear among the stars. And as they got closer, she could smell the burning wood.

Nandina, Mala, and Dusty emerged from the trees into a small clearing. The large fire crackled in front of them. Dozens of people stood around the area. There was the clink of beer bottles and the sound of raucous laughter among the partiers. Low volume country music came from somewhere among the crowd. A line of dense woods stretched behind the scene, giving a backdrop of dark, vertical lines.

A guy that Nandina recognized from the day she had been with her parents at the school was approaching. He was wearing jeans, a plaid button-down shirt, and a blue cap. He lightly punched

Dusty on the chest and then introduced himself to Nandina and Mala. His name was Bartley.

Bartley offered all three of them beers, but, since he was driving, Dusty declined and went with Nandina and Mala as they followed Bartley over to the side of the crowd where he had been sitting on a fallen oak tree. Both of the girls grabbed beers from the cooler on the ground next to the upturned roots that were reaching toward the rest of the woods like grasping fingers.

Pretty soon, Bartley was wrapped up in a conversation with several of his work buddies that had wandered up, and when Mala knew that she was out of his eyesight, she looked at Nandina and mouthed the words, *he is so hot.*

As the night progressed, Nandina felt herself slowly falling into the rhythm of Crow County. It was definitely a lot different from Bishopville, but, so far, she thought that the area was somewhere that she could feel at home.

She already knew that she liked Dusty, and Bartley also seemed like an alright kind of guy. She told herself that as long as she was talking to people and building new friendships, she wouldn't allow herself to think about Jackson.

After Dusty wandered into the woods to pee, Bartley approached the girls again. He immediately began talking to Nandina. He asked her what she thought of her new home so far and what her plans for the summer were.

Mala stood behind Bartley. She was making big, exaggerated eyes at Nandina. Mala nodded her head and winked at Nandina, as if cheering on the exchange between the two.

"What do you think you're doing?" It was a girl's voice that came from behind Nandina.

Nandina turned around to face a girl that had long blonde hair. She was wearing a persimmon-colored blouse. She was obviously drunk. Similar to the way that she had recognized Bartley, Nandina also remembered this girl from the hallway at the school on that same day. That day, the girl had been talking to Dusty. "What?" Nandina asked. She was not trying to sound confrontational. She was just looking for a clarification about what she thought she heard the girl say.

"You know, if I wasn't leaving this place in the fall, it would really bother me what you're doing," the blonde girl rattled off.

So that's what it was, Nandina realized. The girl must have a thing for Bartley, and she didn't want Nandina talking to him. "I'm just being friendly is all," Nandina said and glanced at Bartley, who was backing off from the situation.

"Oh, is that what you call it?" The girl now had her hands on her hips. "Listen, you don't want to have anything to do with him." She nodded past Nandina, toward Bartley.

"What?" This time, the question was from Bartley. "That hurts, Moira," he was holding his clenched fist against his heart. His guy friends were surrounding him, watching the girls and laughing at his expense. Bartley playfully elbowed one of them in the gut.

"Why don't you mind your own business," Mala spoke up from behind Nandina and was taking a step forward.

Oh no, Nandina thought to herself. Here we go. She knew if need be, Mala could, and would, get scrappy.

Moira looked at Mala. Her eyes shot down over the length of her and back up again. "Who are you?"

"I'm her best friend," Mala stated, proudly. "Who are you?"

"Moira Everson." The named rolled off the girl's lips. She stared at Mala for a few seconds before turning her attention back to Nandina. "I'm just saying, watch where you step around here." With that, Moira turned around and began walking away.

The confrontation had put a damper on the rest of the evening.

For the remainder of the night, Mala was spun up about Moira's verbal attack on her friend. And Nandina was just plain confused about the whole thing.

By the time that the three of them made it back to Nandina's house, it was late.

Nandina could tell that her parents had already gone to bed. As Dusty's truck had made its way up the driveway, she had seen that there was only one lamp on in the house. The lamp was on a small, round table next to the front door. It meant that they were asleep.

Nandina led her friends around the side of the house and across the back yard to where an old gazebo sat near the woods.

The white paint on the rails and banisters was chipped, and it had some type of unwanted vines that were growing all over it, but the dilapidated look of the structure only added to its after-midnight allure.

Nandina and Dusty sat on the wooden floor of the gazebo, facing one another, while Mala was sitting against the side, leaning up against one of the posts.

Overhead, the moon shone down on them. The night had turned considerably cooler.

"Sorry about Moira," Dusty said to Nandina.

Nandina shrugged her shoulders. "It's okay. She's just looking out for her friends."

Mala laughed. "Looking out for her friends? She nearly ripped your head off, Nanny. And believe me, for a hot minute out there I thought I was going to have to retaliate."

"I guess she has her own way of trying to make things work out the way that she thinks they should." Dusty had a faraway look in his eyes as he thought about what he was saying and nodded his head. "By saying the wrong things to the wrong people at the wrong time.

Both of the girls laughed at Dusty's description of Moira.

"I thought she just wanted Bartley for herself. That was the impression that I got," Nandina said.

Dusty shook his head. "They used to date, but they broke up earlier this year. She's going away to college in the fall, and I guess Bartley is set on staying here. You could be right though. Maybe she does still want him, and maybe she doesn't even realize it herself."

"Well, in that case, I say, good for her." Mala was relaxed now. She was admiring her recently polished fingernails.

Nandina looked at her friend. "Mala, you just said how you thought you were going to have to fight, and now..."

"I'm just saying it's good to see a girl fight for her man for a change. And look at her anyway. You just said that she is following her dreams and not letting a man hold her back. Well, I say good for her." Mala looked at Nan. "Remember all those stories I used to write when we were little? How the guy always rescued the girl and they lived happily ever after? Maybe it should be the other way around sometimes."

"And what's so wrong with that?" Dusty asked.

"Which part? The guy rescuing the girl or the happily ever after?" Nandina asked.

Dusty shrugged his shoulders. "Both. I like the simplicity of that kind of thing. It has a certain sort of innocence to it."

Mala continued. "All I'm saying, is if I thought a girl was trying to flirt with Will, I'd..." Mala realized that she had spoken too quickly and given away her own secret. "Oh," she said at realizing her goof.

"Mala," Nandina was smiling at her friend's confession, albeit being an accidental one. "Why haven't you told me? Does he know?" Nandina had thought that she had seen a little bit of spark between Mala and Will before, but she didn't think that either of them would ever act on it. That was the funny thing about Mala—she had this big, romantic view of everyone's relationships, but when it came to her own, she was just as clueless as the rest of them on how to handle it.

"Who's Will?" Dusty asked.

It was obvious to Nandina that Mala was embarrassed by the topic.

"He's just this guy I know. Hey, Nanny, did you tell Dusty about the box you found?"

Nandina went along with Mala's suggestion to change the subject but would be sure to ask her about Will again in private. Nandina looked at Dusty.

"So, I found a handwritten story in my room that told about a ghost from that big house down the road. Abandoned Manor, I think it said the house was called. The girl that wrote the story said that the ghost, Fay, comes here sometimes at night, searching for the spirit of her dead lover."

"I've heard of Fay's ghost," Dusty said. "Everybody around here has. It's a local legend, but I've never heard the part about the second ghost. And he's supposed to be here? At this house?"

Nandina shook her head. She pointed toward the woods. "From what I understood, there's supposed to be another set of greenhouses out there. I think they were the original ones back then, in the nineteen twenties. You didn't know about them?"

"I had no idea," Dusty admitted.

"She also found the key," Mala was quick to point out.

Several minutes later, Nandina returned from inside the house where she had been sent by the insistence of both Mala and Dusty. She had the key, two flashlights, and a battery operated lantern in her hands.

She passed one of the flashlights to Dusty.

Mala reached for the lantern and immediately turned it on. "Now, I like this," she said. The glow filled the entire area underneath the gazebo's roof. Mala smiled. She raised the arm that was holding the lantern straight out in front of her in a pose that reminded Nandina of one of those garden statues, the Cavalier.

"Follow me," Mala said and stepped onto the ground.

Nandina and Dusty trailed behind her, and within seconds, all three of them were stepping off the clean lawn and into the thick brush of the woods.

As they walked, the flashlight beams danced around the leaf-strewn ground and threw shadows of the wide tree trunks.

"This reminds me of when we used to go looking for the Lizard Man," Mala said as she was stepping over a particularly thorny bush.

"The Lizard Man?" It was obvious that Dusty was intrigued by the name alone.

Nandina pushed a low-hanging limb out of her way. "Similar to how you have this old ghost story, back in Bishopville we had the Lizard Man. He was supposedly spotted somewhere around Scape Ore Swamp back in the nineteen eighties. He's supposed to be this scaly humanoid creature. And as ridiculous as it sounds, I used to be terrified of that whole thing."

Dusty shook his head. "I used to be mortified of another legend that we have around here, the bag man, but now I know he's not real. In a way, it's kind of disappointing, don't you think? To find out that those kinds of things aren't real?"

Mala stopped and turned around to face them. The lantern light gave her a spooky, ominous glow. "I hate to be Little Miss Debbie Downer right now, but have y'all forgotten something? Like the fact that there might be a serial killer somewhere out there? And if I've ever seen a place that screams *serial killer*, that has got to be it." She turned back around, holding her lantern high and pointed directly ahead with her other hand.

Two greenhouses stood in front of them. They were not the metal framed ones that Nandina was used to. These had been constructed out of boards. The framework was gray from age and decades of being out in the elements. The plastic sides of the greenhouses were ripped in places and tattered in others. The buildings were in worse shape than what they had been in the photo that Nandina had found in the shoebox; the photo that she assumed had been taken in the 1980s by that Kelly Brighton girl.

Vines grew up the sides and over the tops. With her flashlight, Nandina could see purple flowers that were scattered about the vines. She knew that they were morning glories.

"Morning glories are symbolic of returning love," Mala told them. "They say that, since the flowers bloom in the morning and die by nightfall with new ones replacing the dead ones the following day, the plant is representative of love's endurance."

Above the door was a metal sign. Nandina shined her flashlight on it. The sign had one word stamped into it—PERENNIALS.

"Well, this is it," Nandina reached into her front jeans pocket and pulled out the skeleton key.

Surprisingly, the key easily slid into the lock.

After unlocking it, Nandina pushed on the door, but, because of the thick vine cover, it didn't budge. She pushed harder until it opened far enough for them to go in.

The interior of the greenhouse was littered with dry leaves that had blown in through the ripped plastic sides. Similar to what she had seen on the outside, morning glory vines were running rampant all along the wall and across the floor. At the far end, a fan with large rusted blades rested solemnly in the wall.

Nandina looked up, wanting to take in everything about the place that she could, and was in awe by what she saw above her. Instead of plastic, the ceiling had been constructed with window panes. There were vines and a settling of leaves on the other side, but she was still able to see the stars and the moon.

Next to where she stood, Nandina ran her hands along one of the wooden counter tops. FB AND AF FOREVER was scratched into the wood.

She could imagine Fay and Ambrose lying there on a blanket, holding on to one another as they stared at the night sky.

She traced her fingertips over the carved letters. In a new vision, it was daytime. Orange sunlight tore in through the siding and windows. The countertops and floor were full of trays of blooming flowers. Baskets of petunias hung along the length of the overhead cross bars. The fan at the back of the greenhouse slowly turned. Fay, who was wearing a blue dress, was sitting on the counter where trays of flowers had been shoved aside. She had her legs wrapped around Ambrose, who stood in front of her. They were kissing. Their foreheads and necks glistened from both the humidity of the greenhouse and the passion that they shared.

"I found something over here." In the opposite corner from where Nandina had been wrapped up in the fantasy, Mala placed the lantern on the counter. She bent over to pick up something, and when she stood back up, she placed a metal box next to the lantern. The old hinges screeched when she opened the lid.

By then, both Nandina and Dusty were standing behind Mala, looking over her shoulders.

It was a box of old postcards. All of the pictures were of flowers and greenhouses, in which some of them had people standing in front, while others were solely of the building. Mala flipped the top card over. There was neat, cursive handwriting on the back. She held it closer so that she could see it and read it out loud.

"My dearest Fay, I know in my heart that our love is like perennials. Sometimes, it may seem lost forever, but I know that one day it will return. – A"

Mala lowered the postcard, put it back in the box, and flipped another one over. It too had a handwritten note on the back. She thumbed through the whole stack. They all did.

"These are their love notes," she said, amazed at the enchantment of what she had found. "Whoa, this is epic."

Mala's enthusiasm about Fay and Ambrose's love affair didn't surprise Nandina in the least, but she was taken aback by her own sense of fervor.

Had she been getting wrapped up in the love story just as Mala was? It was unlike her to feel swept away by something like that. She hadn't felt that way about a silly love story in years. Upon first learning about the story, she had wondered if it had all been made up, but now she wasn't so sure.

As soon as they got back in the house, Mala flung herself onto the couch. "I am beat," she said and picked up the TV remote. She flipped through the channels, eventually stopping on a romantic comedy.

Nandina sat beside Mala, staring blankly at the saga that was unfolding on the screen. Dusty was in the chair in the corner.

When Nandina looked at Mala, she saw that she was sound asleep with her feet propped on the coffee table and her phone held in her hands like she was in mid-text.

"I need to be heading out," Dusty said and stood from the chair.

Nandina walked with him to his truck. In the distance, a rooster called.

"What time is it?" Dusty asked, looking around at the sky. "Roosters are supposed to crow at daybreak. It's still dark."

Nandina looked at her watch. "Four-thirty," she said. "It's still two hours 'til morning. I guess somebody needs to get their rooster a better clock."

Dusty laughed and opened his truck door. "See you tomorrow?"

Nandina nodded her head, affirming his request.

Without another word, or moment of hesitation, Dusty leaned toward her and kissed her on the lips.

For a brief moment, Nandina's hand went to his shirt, ready to grasp at the fabric, but just as her fingertips met the cotton, she thought of Jackson. It just didn't seem right kissing somebody else. She pulled back and, with her hand, gently pushed Dusty away.

"Dusty," she said. "Don't."

She could tell that what she had done had hurt Dusty's feelings. He climbed into the driver's seat of the truck, and, with his hand on the door, he looked at her one more time. "I'm sorry," he said. "I shouldn't have done that. Can I still see you tomorrow?"

"Yeah, I'll see you tomorrow."

And Dusty slammed the truck door, leaving Nandina alone with her thoughts.

"NANNY, YOU HAVE got to get your butt up."

Nandina opened her eyes. Mala, who had taken her contacts out for the night, was looking down at her from behind a pair of round, black-framed glasses. Underneath a long, knitted house sweater, Mala was wearing a set of loose fitting Valentine's Day pajamas that had little red hearts printed all over them.

"What time is it?" Nandina groaned and, with squinted eyes, looked toward the clock that was on her nightstand. The room was too bright with early morning sunlight. By the tone of Mala's urging voice, it was obvious to Nandina that she had been trying for a while to wake her up.

"It's eight o'clock, but that's not the point." With the remote, Mala turned on the TV and flung herself backward onto the bed. She landed right next to Nandina. "You have got to see this."

Eight o'clock, Nandina thought with agony. Three hours of sleep is nowhere near enough.

On the TV, there was the crackle of microphones at a live press conference.

A law officer approached the podium that had been set up in the front of the room. "There has been another confirmed murder," he stated matter-of-factly. The caption that was at the bottom of the screen stated that the officer's name was Richard Tomlin. "This time, however, the murder is out of my jurisdiction, but I will continue to be working closely with the case as it progresses."

Before going on, Tomlin looked down at the paper that he had in front of him.

"This morning at approximately seven o'clock, in downtown Columbia, a city maintenance worker found the body of college student Liana Vine, who had been stabbed to death. Due to circumstances that seem to be very similar to the murder of Mary Gold last weekend, we do, at this point in time, feel confident that this is the work of a serial killer. Being that we have two very broad age groups, age does not appear to play a factor in who the killer may target next. We will keep you updated as this is a still developing case. Thank you."

All around the room, there was the sound of questions being asked from the reporters, but Tomlin walked off the stage.

Similar to the way the murder scene of Mary Gold had been found, this one, according to the auburn-haired news reporter that stood on the city sidewalk, had a tangle of vines where Liana's body had been discovered.

They had hoped that the first murder had been an isolated case, but with the news of a second victim, Nandina and Mala became more concerned.

It was also a little thrilling.

When it came time for Mala to leave, Nandina, Tom, and Rose all insisted that she call them when she got safely to Bishopville.

"And when were you going to tell me about you and Will?" Nandina wanted to know.

"It's just something that we're keeping on the quiet side right now." Mala told her. "But I was going to let you know sooner or later."

Not long after Mala was gone, Nandina laid down on the couch and, due to her lack of sleep the night before, she quickly fell into slumber. She had a dream in which she walked into the greenhouse early one morning. To her horror, she discovered Dusty's bloody body lying dead on the floor atop a thick mound of dusty miller plants that had been yanked up from the soil, roots and all.

AS PROMISED, NANDINA met up with Dusty later that day. They decided that they would go to The Crow's Nest. The restaurant was located in what looked like an old house with a front porch that stretched across its entire width.

Multi-colored Christmas lights were draped in the trees that surrounded the small, dirt parking lot. There was a screen door that led inside. Throughout most of the year, the windows of the restaurant were open and had screens that would keep the mosquitoes and flies out. Inside, a long bar took up one wall, and a series of booths were along the other.

The place was decorated with various crow related knick-knacks. There was even a large, inflatable crow with red eyes that had served as a marketing tool for the not-so-classic horror movie, Talons, that hung in the corner and loomed over the crowd.

A framed, bright blue poster board from the year that the football team had won the state championship hung near the door. GO JHA CARRION! It read. The sign had been autographed by every team member and cheerleader, and it had hung in the same spot for over a decade.

Despite the first impression, The Crow's Nest was actually much nicer than it let on to be. For example, in addition to the salt and pepper, each table had several other shakers that held various dried herbs—basil, oregano, chives, rosemary, and thyme.

In a corner booth, Nandina sat across from Dusty. They were talking about things that they liked.

"I used to love going out into the swamp and catching crawfish back in Bishopville. It was something that I did all the time with my friends."

She told Dusty how, when she had been little, catching crawfish was something that her entire family did together. She, her parents, and her grandmother, Lily, would go to the swamp and catch as many as they could over the course of one afternoon. Afterward, they would take them to Lily's house where they were cooked in a large pot in the backyard. They all stood around enormous, upright spools to eat.

"Those were some of the most magical summer nights of my life," she said.

After leaving The Crow's Nest, Dusty drove her out to Pritchard's Pond.

The large pond was owned by an old man named John Pritchard. It sat on the back portion of his land, way back from his house. Even though the pond was privately owned, most people that fished around the area were allowed by Mr. Pritchard to go to the pond any time that they wanted, whether previously announced or otherwise, despite the posted signs that read PRIVATE PROPERTY – NO TRESPASSING.

The pond finally appeared in front of them. Even though it had been over a year since Dusty had seen it, it was just like he remembered. The banks and surrounding fields were overgrown with tall grass. Cattails stood upright along the muddy edge.

Nan opened her door and stepped out of the truck. As soon as her feet hit the ground, she took a deep breath and inhaled the clean, country air.

Dusty got out of the truck and joined her by the pond.

That day, he told her about how he and his best friend, Tyler, used to love to go out to the pond fishing.

He told her about how Tyler had died the previous winter.

As Dusty opened up more to Nandina, the longing that she felt to be back with Jackson seemed to drift further away.

THE CROW COUNTY tractor pull was held every July 4th weekend at the County Fairgrounds that, as far as Nandina could tell, was never used for anything else.

That year, Nandina went with Dusty, Mala, and Will. It was going to be Bartley's inaugural year competing in the adult category. It was the first time that she had ever been to a tractor pull, and she had no idea what to expect.

The sun was setting over the outdoor arena that was made of red dirt and mud. American flags were hanging across the backs of the bleachers. There was a cinderblock concession stand on each side. The spotlights that were shining onto the dirt track were some of the brightest that Nandina had ever seen.

After the sun was down, the main event started. Nandina quickly caught on that it was the tractor that could pull a weighted sled the furthest was the winner. Black smoke poured out of the tractor mufflers. When it came time for Bartley to go, Nandina, Dusty, Mala, and Will stood and cheered him on. In the end, he finished third place.

After the competition, a wooden trailer that was draped all the way around with red, white, and blue sashes was pulled out onto the center of the track. Two girls were sitting on a box. They were each wearing elegant gowns. One of the girls was Moira. She was wearing a silver crown.

The Pull Queen pageant had been held the night before. It was tradition for the previous year's winner to crown the new Queen at the end of the tractor pull.

After the trailer stopped, the new Pull Queen was announced over the speaker system, and Moira removed the crown from her head and placed it on top of the brunette's carefully styled hair. Moira was all smiles as she passed on the legacy to someone new.

When the crowning was complete, the tractor pulled the trailer off the track where it disappeared through a cloud of smoke.

Fireworks began to shoot off from the north side of the track, and received thunderous applause from the audience.

Out of the corner of her eye, Nandina saw Mala and Will kiss underneath the multi-colored sparkles in the sky.

THE NEXT DAY, there was the picture of yet another murder victim. This particular one shook the teenagers to the core. Now, neither age *nor* gender appeared to be a factor. His name was Dill Weed. He had only been eighteen years old.

Seeing the photo of him on the TV, Nandina couldn't help but think about the uncertainty of life. Dill, for example, had been taken way before his time.

For some reason, the image of Moira passing on her pageant crown to the other girl replayed itself in Nandina's mind. She remembered how happy Moira had looked that night at the tractor pull. To Nandina, the event seemed symbolic of Moira putting her past behind her and moving forward. And maybe, Nandina thought, that was what *she* needed to do as well.

She couldn't believe that she was feeling inspired by Moira of all people, but just maybe Moira was the bravest of them all. Moira was, after all, the one that was gutsy enough to chase after her dreams.

NANDINA WANTED TO do something special for Dusty. She knew that his favorite color was dark blue and that he liked anything that had the state emblem of a palmetto tree and a crescent moon, but a t-shirt, license plate, or decal wouldn't do. She wanted to go big. Ultimately, she came up with the perfect idea.

On a scorching day at the end of July, Nandina walked behind the old greenhouses. The purple and blue flowers on the morning glory vines were open. She was eyeballing the amount of space that was available. She was trying to get an idea if she could get her father's small tractor back there.

Deciding that she could, she went into the shed and climbed onto the tractor seat.

She had briefly considered asking Bartley to help her, but decided against it. As it turned out, driving the tractor wasn't as difficult as she thought it would be. The hardest part was just a matter of learning the clutch and the throttle.

She had to drive around the thickest part of the woods and enter the clearing from the back. Behind the perennial house, she dug a hole with the scoop that was on the front of the tractor.

Then, back at the new greenhouses, there was a line of palmetto trees for sale along the south-facing wall. She picked out the one she wanted. It was a shorter, thinner one, and she chained it to the back of the tractor.

She dragged the tree around to where she had dug. She pulled the tree across the ground until it fell in the hole. She had to jump down from the seat and move the chain closer to the top of the tree, but this time, when she moved the tractor forward, the chain pulled taught, and the tree stood upright.

To fill the hole and pack the dirt, she used a shovel. In the humidity, she was covered in dirt and sweat by the time that she was done. It was a good thing that she had worn an old t-shirt and jeans.

She put the tractor back under the shed and was showered by the time her parents got home.

When Dusty got there, Nandina met him on the front porch. She had decided to wear a dress that was Dusty's favorite color, dark blue, a pair of cowboy boots, and a silver chain that she had run through the end of the skeleton key that went to the greenhouse.

It made her smile to see that Dusty had worn his favorite shirt that had the state emblem on the back.

"I want to show you something," she told him and led him around the house. There were lightning bugs hovering above the green grass. They walked past the gazebo where Nandina picked up the battery operated lantern that she had left sitting there just for this occasion. It was the same lantern that Mala had carried on their previous journey to the greenhouses. Nandina turned the lantern on and they stepped into the woods.

When they got to the greenhouses, Nandina unlocked the door. She grabbed Dusty's hand and led him inside. The look on his face when he saw the blue blanket that she had draped over the wooden countertop sent her heart racing.

Still holding onto his hand, Nandina placed the fingertips from her other hand underneath his chin and tilted his head up.

Through the old windowpane that was directly above them, that night's crescent moon was visible in the night sky. The moon hung next to the top of the palmetto tree that stood there. She had even run an extension cord from the back porch of the house to the top of the greenhouse where a dim spotlight was plugged in that illuminated the tree in a soft glow.

When Dusty tore his attention away from the picturesque scene, Nandina pulled him to her, and their lips met in tandem.

Nandina spun Dusty around and eased him backward onto the blanket.

Dusty obliged and scooted himself all the way up so that he was lying on his back, letting Nandina crawl on top of him

When she was where she wanted to be, she was pulling at his clothes. Underneath her dress, Dusty's hands were moving slowly over her flesh.

Later, when their heart rates began to return to normal, they were both staring through the overhead window.

"Nandina, where have you been? I have been frantic!"

Her mother was standing on the back porch when Nandina emerged from the woods with Dusty.

"We were just hanging out," Nandina said. "It's no big deal."

"It *is* a big deal, Nandina." Her mother spun her head around to face Dusty. "And how dare you take her out in the woods at this time of the night."

"He didn't do anything," Nandina stated defensively. "I did it. I took him out there."

Now her mother's pulse was visibly thrumming in her throat.

Nandina wondered if her mother had seen that she was wearing Dusty's necklace, and, if so, if she knew what it signified was between them.

"There has been another murder," her mother said. "This time, only thirty miles from here. It was a lady named Kimberly Fern. You have no idea how worried I was." She looked back to Dusty. "Good night, Dusty."

10.

I WOKE UP with the sun glaring through the room's west-facing window. It took a moment for my mind to register where I was. At first, I thought that I was at home, but then I remembered that I had spent the night at Bartley's house.

I was so worried over both Rose's comatose state and the killer that I had barely slept the night before. My mind had been racing over the details of the past several months.

I rolled over on the couch and saw that Bartley was already gone. I knew that he was expected to report to work promptly at eight o'clock every morning. I picked up my phone to see what time it was. It was just a little after nine. I had a new text message from Nan.

I'm going to be staying at Bartley's house too.
I can't stay at the hospital forever. I'll visit Mom after school and on the weekends, but the police want me to stay there during the week. One good thing is that I'll be right down the hall from you :)

Something clicked in my head and it made sense to me then. *That* was why I had been stuck in the room with Bartley. It was so that Nan could have the guest room for herself. And really, I liked the idea of her being with me.

By the time that I made my way downstairs, I discovered that I was alone in the house. Not only had Bartley left to go to work, but so had Mr. and Mrs. Vance.

I wandered into the kitchen and looked around for something that I could have for breakfast. I hadn't really eaten the night before, and I was famished. After finding the refrigerator and pantry nearly empty of anything that looked quick, the only options had been fried chicken or cookies, I reached out my hand for one of the apples in a large bowl on the countertop when I noticed a yellow piece of paper. It was a note from Bartley's mom that had been stuck next to one of those purple pepper-spray key rings.

Dusty, there's leftover fried chicken in the fridge. I put some pepper spray out for you. Don't be afraid to use it if need be! Make yourself at home. You know you're always welcomed here!

- Pam

I lowered the piece of paper and glanced across the kitchen. Through the open bar area that connected the two rooms, I could see Mr. Vance's gun cabinet in the living room.

It was an enormous glass-fronted piece of Civil War era furniture. The rifles and shotguns were lined neatly inside. Weighing my options, I looked at the purple pepper-spray key ring and rolled my eyes. I knew, without a doubt, that if anything even remotely scary happened, I was going for the guns.

I looped the key ring over my left ring finger, bit into the apple, held it in my mouth between my teeth, and grabbed an OJ from the fridge with my free hand. I carried it all back upstairs where I changed from my sleep clothes into my running shorts and shirt.

No, I didn't go running. I'm not stupid. I had been instructed by both of my parents and the police to stay inside. I mean, the whole point of me being at the Vance's house was so that no one knew where I was.

So instead of running out on the road, where I would be out in the open, I was hitting the treadmill that morning.

The Vance's had a basement that they had transformed half of into a home gym, and there was a bar area that had a large, yellow sectional couch and a big screen TV.

The gym was about the size of my bedroom at home. They had a weight bench, a treadmill, and one of those things that you use to work on your shoulders. The gym wasn't one of those that is rarely used. All three of the Vances used it regularly. They were in great shape.

I stepped onto the treadmill. There was a TV mounted on the wall across from the bulky exercise equipment. I tried to watch TV as I ran, but the local news was covered with the story of the serial killer. I couldn't watch. I had to turn it off.

"WE HAVE REASON to believe that the person that attacked Mrs. Bush is a copycat." The officer sat across from Nan and I at the Vance's large kitchen table.

Colby, who had driven Nan from the hospital, had already headed back to Bishopville.

I recognized the officer as being the same one that had her pistol pointed at me the day before when I had come down the embankment next to the Bush's property. According to the name badge on her dark blue uniform, her last name was Wooley. She had her dark brown hair pulled back in a ponytail.

"A copycat means that there is someone imitating another killer," Wooley explained.

I wondered if Nan and I looked confused to her or if Wooley just felt the need to explain everything to us. I nodded my head, "I know what being a copycat means." I didn't intend to sound like such a smart ass, but I mean, really.

Wooley continued. "There was another murder last night. Have y'all seen it on the news?"

I shook my head, remembering that I had turned the TV off when the story came on earlier that morning.

Wooley slid a photo across the table and stopped it right in front of us. When I looked down, I saw a man that must have been in his mid to late thirties. He looked serious in the picture, like he was a college professor or something. Something about it looked like a publicity photo, similar to one of an author on the back of a book's dust-jacket.

"Pete Moss," she said. "He was murdered last night at approximately nine o'clock." Wooley then shook her head as if she was correcting me, but I hadn't said a word. "It was over two hundred miles away from here. Yeah, the killer could've traveled that far in that amount of time, sure, but here's the kicker."

She slid another photo toward me. This one was a middle-aged woman with red hair.

"Scarlett Oak," she said. "Murdered yesterday afternoon. We have evidence of her buying groceries at five-thirty in the afternoon. Her body was found at six-fifteen. Rose's attack is approximated to have taken place within that same time frame. Scarlett Oak was ninety miles from here, in the opposite direction. There is just no way that the same person did all of this. One thing we're not ruling out is the possibility of this being a domestic case."

"Did you know that Rose and her brother-in-law, Colby, like the cheese, have a—um—history together?" she asked us.

In all honesty, I did not know that. And frankly, I wished that I never did. I looked at Nan.

My mind began to spin a scenario where Rose would be attacked. What I was picturing playing out in my mind was exactly what Officer Wooley had suggested, that Tom was the one that attacked Rose. He had found out about the affair and snapped, hitting his wife against the head because he was beyond angry. He then "discovered" her comatose body and called the police.

Was that why she was wearing that nice black dress that afternoon? Was she on her way to see Colby?

As my mind rambled, something else occurred to me. What if it was Colby that hit her? It was possible. Maybe she wanted to end the affair, but Colby was obsessed with her, so much so that *he* was the one that came undone.

"That was a long time ago," Nan said defensively. "It was before I was born. I know this has nothing to do with Colby."

"We're just looking at this from every angle. No one is accusing anybody of anything, Nandina."

Wooley barely gave us enough time for all of this new information to sink in when she reached into the side pocket on her pants and pulled out a plastic bag. She opened the bag, removed the contents, and slammed what was inside onto the table right in front of me. I couldn't see what it was just yet, but the sound that it had made when it hit the table was undeniably one of metal.

She slid her hand away in a magician-like maneuver to reveal what was underneath.

I recognized it immediately and knew that Nan did as well.

It was the skeleton key to the old greenhouse.

Seeing the key as a piece of evidence in an attempted murder case caused my skin to crawl.

"We found this at the crime scene late yesterday evening. I don't know how we missed it on our first sweep through but we did. When I saw it, it was lying in the dirt near where Mrs. Bush had been found. I think she had it with her that day. Maybe it is a key, no pun intended, in the *why* of this case. Do you have any idea what the key goes to? It says *Perennials* on the tag, so it would make sense that it is the key to one of the greenhouses, but we tried, and it doesn't fit any of them."

"There are two more greenhouses in the woods behind the house. It goes to one of those," Nan said. "The key was in an old shoebox that I found in my room."

I thought about that night that Nandina took me out there. I wondered if Wooley knew about how

Rose had been mad at us that night because she hadn't been able to find us.

This mention of finding the key inside the shoebox obviously perked Wooley's attention. "Was there anything else *with* the key?"

"There was a handwritten ghost story about our house and Abandoned Manor. It was like it was a school paper or something, and some old photos, but..."

"I think I'm going to need to see what you're talking about."

KELLY BRIGHTON MADDOX was a heavy-set woman with short dark hair. She was wearing a shirt that had huge garnet rhinestones across the front of the collar. Her earrings matched the color of the stones.

There was a second officer that guided Kelly into the police station's small break room that Rebecca Wooley was using. The room smelled like stale, burnt coffee. There was a refrigerator with a microwave on top, and a coffee pot that sat on one of two fold-out card tables. The other table held the zebra-printed notebook from Nandina's bedroom, the lined pages that the ghost story had been written on, and the shoebox. The box was open so that the photos could be seen.

There was something about the story that had grabbed Rebecca's attention—the mystery about the proprietor of Abandoned Manor. Since it appeared that Rose had been carrying the greenhouse key with her that day, Rebecca felt certain that all of this was connected to the assault that had ultimately placed Rose into a coma.

After reading the story, it had taken a while for Rebecca to locate Kelly. It was no surprise to Rebecca that, in the intervening years since she had written the story, Kelly Brighton had gotten married and was now Kelly Maddox.

"Kelly, my name is Rebecca Wooley." Rebecca was standing behind the table that held the items from Kelly's teenage years. "I'm just going to ask you a few questions. Do you recognize anything that you see here on this table?"

Kelly looked over the items and nodded her head. "I recognize all of it. Where did you find this stuff?" She sounded nostalgic. "It was a school project that I was working on."

"It was left behind at your old house. A young lady, who currently lives in the house and she has your old room I guess, found it underneath the radiator." Wooley picked up the notebook paper. "Now, to get the details for this story that you wrote, how many people did you talk to?"

"Not many. Most of that information you can find on file at the library, but I did talk to a couple, just to give the story a personal touch."

"You mentioned in here that there was somebody that you talked to that wished to remain anonymous. Can you tell me who that person was?"

Kelly shrugged her shoulders. "I don't know. You have to understand, all of that was a long time ago. I can't remember what his name was. I just remember that he was an elderly man, so I'm sure he's not still alive now."

"Besides describing the party that his parents went to, do you remember if he said anything that you thought was a little bit odd or out of the ordinary?"

Kelly nodded her head. "He did. He told me that there was a rumor that Fay, she was the Blade girl that got shot, was pregnant. That was why she was locked up in the house for all those months. She wasn't sick like everybody said. I didn't put it in my paper because my daddy told me not to. He said that all of that was just speculation, and that it was none of my business."

"And you've never told anyone about this?"

"No ma'am. I was fourteen at the time. I figured that all of that stuff would be figured out by the adults. And to be honest with you, I don't think I've even thought about any of this for the past thirty years. You don't think I'm withholding information, do you? Because..."

"Nobody thinks you're withholding information. Did he say that she was pregnant when she died?"

"Oh, no," she said. "He firmly believed that Fay had the baby before that night. He said that after Fay's death, the baby was put up for adoption."

After Kelly left, Rebecca called a genealogist that she knew. She requested a rundown that would follow both Fay and Hayley Blade's bloodlines all the way from 1925 to the present.

Later, when the genealogist called her back, Rebecca could hardly believe what she heard.

One of the ancestors, the one from Hayley's lineage, was Pam Vance. And the other, the one from Fay's, the murdered Blade sister, was Jennifer Braxton.

If anybody had reason to kill over an inheritance that would be worth a fortune, it was somebody that had started out with nothing, Rebecca thought. Somebody just like Jennifer Braxton.

11.

"CANCELLED! THE PARTY is off," Mrs. Vance was telling her husband.

Nan and I were upstairs in the guest bedroom. It was the room that Nan was going to be sleeping in that night. The overhead light was off, but in the corner, a single lamp was turned on, giving just the right amount of glow to our surroundings.

We were sitting on the floor, playing some kind of lame board game that we had found shoved underneath the guest room bed earlier in the day. The object of the game was, by the roll of dice, to move your game piece all the way around the board while avoiding and overcoming certain obstacles that stood in your way. Both the box and the board itself were discolored with age. Some of the cards were stained with what I assumed was fruit punch. For the life of me, I can't think of what the game was called.

We could hear the conversation between Mr. and Mrs. Vance that was going on in the living room, which was located right at the bottom of the stairs.

"Pam, we've already spent the money. We can't back out now," William Vance told his wife.

"William, I just don't think it's right. It doesn't seem like we should be having a party with everything else that's going on. And what about the rain? Have you even *looked* at the weather?"

I couldn't answer for Mr. Vance, but I'll admit that I, for one, hadn't even so much as given the weather a fleeting thought.

Apparently, there was a band of heavy storm clouds that was expected to wreak havoc across the state. The storms were supposed to last throughout the night with the brunt of the activity in the early evening hours, just when the party would have been getting underway.

"Honey, everybody thinks we should go ahead with it. Even Tom texted me earlier today and said *do it*."

William, we are *not* having the party, and that is the final word on the subject. I don't want to hear anything else about it. We can always reschedule for later."

"What about the announcement?" William asked. "When will we make it public?"

"Is that *all* you care about?"

RAIN WAS POURING down. To Deputy Rebecca Wooley, the road seemed like a river, and her car was a boat that was sailing through. An illustration from a Greek mythology book flashed through her mind. It was one of an old gondola on the river, Styx, as it transported the dead to Hades.

To prevent the car from hydroplaning, Rebecca had to drive slowly, but, even then, the rotating tires still caused a wave of water that was as high as the windows.

Rebecca was certain that she was on the right train of thought in the process of solving the crime—Jenny Braxton was the person that was guilty of assaulting Rose Bush. The motive had something to do with the inheritance of Abandoned Manor and a nearly hundred year old ghost story. But why did Rose have the greenhouse key with her that day? And more importantly, why did it matter enough for Jenny to try and kill her?

After Rebecca was done with the investigation, Jenny would, more than likely, be charged with attempted manslaughter. In the event that Rose ended up dying from the attack, the charge would be increased to murder.

And then I'm retiring from all of this, Rebecca thought. This will be my final case, and solving it will send me out in style. Then I'll be sitting in the back yard reading cozy mysteries with a nice glass of red wine in my hand.

With the tale of the two censured lovers, the key to the place that they would meet in secret, an inheritance, and Jenny being the ancestor of Fay Blade and Ambrose Fletcher, not to mention Jenny's spotty and sordid past, all of the elements seemed to be in place for Rebecca's grand finale off the police force.

Rebecca had steered the car off the main road and she was driving down the long, flooded red dirt drive that stretched through the rows of the Braxton's pecan trees. That year, since Mr. Braxton was no longer part of the household or business, the pecan farm had fallen into neglect.

Usually, as harvest time neared, the grasses and weeds around the base of each of the trees were burnt back with a restricted-use herbicide in order to make spotting and gathering the fallen pecans easier. But that year it hadn't been done, and the pecans, when they fell, got lost in the overgrowth.

It wasn't only what was at ground level that had slipped into neglect. The webworm caterpillars within the tree branches were terrible that fall. In Ryan's absence, no one had tried to keep them under control, and the worms had built so many nests among the branches that, in the current dark and rainy night, they resembled cheap Halloween decor.

After the police car crested the final incline of the driveway, it emerged through the other side of the pecan orchard. Rebecca was shocked about what she saw in front of her. She remembered the last time that she had been out to the Braxton house had been on the night that the outside brick wall had been vandalized with the word *Murderer* spray painted in bold, red letters across the front.

And now, the newer part of the Braxton house had been demolished. Brick and board lay in several, triangular piles around the surviving structure like they were funeral pyres. The sturdy wooden shutters that had been attached to each side of the windows were propped against one of the piles of brick. The windows, with their glass still intact, were lying flat on the ground in a neat stack. A large, yellow bulldozer was parked behind the rubble.

What was left standing on the lot was a small house with a blue door.

Looking at the scene from behind the car's windshield where the wipers were struggling to keep up with the amount of rain that was falling, Rebecca's memory took her back to the night over a year earlier when she had last been there. Back then, the blue door that she was seeing now had been inside the house. It had led into the Braxton's master bedroom. Rebecca remembered it clearly because she'd had to go through that same door to get a statement from Jenny about the vandalism that had taken place on their property. Jenny had been drunk that night, just as she would be now, Rebecca thought.

Rebecca was old enough to remember the original house that had stood vacant on the property for years before the newly married Ryan and Jennifer Braxton moved into it, fresh out of high school. Rebecca had thought that the house had been tiny and barely livable for two people, much less three as it became evident that Jenny was carrying a baby. For the next couple of years, the family had lived in the house but added on to the original structure turning it into a ranch-style home.

The structure that she was looking at now, illuminated by her car's headlights, was the original house that the Braxtons had, at one time, called home. She turned the car off, pulled the hood of her poncho over her head, and stepped out into the rain.

She ran the short distance from her car to the house.

At some point in time, Jenny had hung a wooden, heart-shaped wreath on the front of the blue door. The wreath was hand pained and had a little plaque with the words HOME SWEET HOME across the front.

Recently, someone had planted yellow and purple pansies around the perimeter of the "new" house. The flower beds were almost black with newly turned dirt and garden soil.

Rebecca knocked, and, from the other side of the door, she heard Jenny call out.

"Come in!" Jenny's voice was scratchy and hoarse. "It's unlocked!" she yelled.

Rebecca hesitantly turned the knob and pushed the door open.

Inside the house, candlelight flickered against the darkness causing shadows to dance and jump across the room.

The space that she walked into was hard to comprehend in the half-dark.

The small area that she stood in was cramped with a sofa, two end-tables, and an entertainment center that had a flat screen TV resting on top. Straight ahead was a makeshift wall of board and sheetrock that had been sloppily hammered together. Rebecca could see the end of the bed that was poking out on the other side of the wall. The bathroom was to the left, and to the right, through the door that used to lead to the large walk-in closet, Rebecca spotted the corner of a stove that had been left sitting askance on the floor. The wall that separated the living room from the kitchen was partially demolished. A wide, gaping hole was there, and Rebecca could see the plaster and the wooden studs that had electrical wires running up and down them. A large, heavy sledge hammer was leaning against the wall on the floor below the hole.

Despite all of the detail that she was taking in about her surroundings, Rebecca didn't see Jenny anywhere in the bedlam that was before her.

"Have a seat." The voice was sudden and had come from behind Rebecca, catching her off guard. The intonation caused Rebecca's skin to crawl.

Rebecca spun around and saw that Jenny had been right behind her all along, and just inches from where she stood. When Rebecca took a step back without paying attention, she nearly tripped over an orange extension cord that snaked dangerously across the floor. She lost her footing but caught herself on the arm of the couch. It was then that she was able to get a better look at Jenny.

Jenny Braxton was sitting in a plastic lawn chair. Her too-thin frame was draped in a yellow rain jacket. Her hair had been chopped off. It looked like she had done it herself. It was hard to tell, but, in the candlelight, her hair looked almost black. Rebecca, like most, knew that Jenny had always dyed her hair that horrible color of bleach-blonde, but had never once considered what the woman's natural color would be. The candlelight sent a combination of orange light and shadow across Jenny's face that caused her to look grotesque. Monster-like.

Rebecca slid her bottom from the arm of the couch down to the seat. After she was situated, she realized that it wasn't just the light that was playing tricks on her; there was something *wrong* with Jenny's face.

There was a rash that spread from the bridge of Jenny's nose onto each of her cheeks. Rebecca thought that the shape of the affliction closely resembled that of a butterfly.

Jenny must have been able to see the look that Rebecca was giving her because she was quick to offer an explanation. "Lupus," she said.

That explained a lot. The disease was why Jenny had become so gaunt over the years. An extreme sensitivity to sunlight was why Jenny would sometimes go weeks at a time without venturing out in the daylight. It was why her hair had become so thin.

"You're going to believe what you want to believe," Jenny said. "But I didn't drink while I was pregnant with Tyler. I've had a drinking problem before, but not then. All of that stuff is gossip and hearsay. And all of those things you've probably heard about me doing meth isn't true." She was shaking her head. Her speech was slurred. Rebecca could tell that the woman in front of her was drunk. "I've never once messed with that. When bad things happen, people look for somewhere to place the blame. I was an easy target. Everybody in Crow County believed it. Hell, even my own husband began to think it was true. I guess he had heard so much of it that he didn't know what to believe anymore."

Jenny's voice cracked in the otherwise quiet house. They were surrounded by the eerie kind of quiet that is achievable only when the power is out and when there's not even the hum of the refrigerator and other electronic equipment as barely-there background noise.

"I was nineteen when I had Tyler," Jenny said. "Back then was the happiest that I had ever been, and it was right here in this house." She looked around at her surroundings.

Even in the candlelit darkness, Rebecca could decipher in Jenny's eyes a look of longing for days gone by. Rebecca understood why Jenny had torn down the rest of the house. It was her way of crawling into the past and to a happier time in her life.

"Inside this little house I was completely and totally happy. Probably, to most people, it looked like I had nothing. For me, it felt like I had the world. I had a husband that I loved dearly and a new baby on the way. We were going to be a family. For nine or ten months, I didn't drink anything. I thought that I was over it, and I painted that door blue in an effort to keep the bad things out for good." She nodded her head toward the door that was still standing open, offering a view of the outside darkness where the rain was still coming down in sheets.

"I read somewhere that the color blue is believed to keep out the evil spirits. I thought that it would work, but I guess they found their way in anyway. I still yell for them to get out, but they don't always listen. They are monkeys on my back that I just can't seem to get rid of."

"These evil spirits—you said that you see them?"

Jenny nodded her head. "Oh, yeah," she said. There's one right there." She pointed to the floor beside the couch where Rebecca was sitting.

At the uncanny notion, Rebecca felt the hairs on the back of her neck stand on end. She looked to where Jenny was pointing but didn't see anything. "What do they look like?" she asked quizzically.

"I already told you. Monkeys," Jenny said.

An image of a red-eyed and fanged spider monkey, with his long tail swishing behind him as he slinked across the floor, popped into Wooley's head. She had to shake off the chills that the thought gave her. "Have you been drinking tonight, Mrs. Braxton?"

Jenny laughed and picked up an amber colored bottle that was sitting on the floor next to her chair. "I quit," Jenny said and held the empty bottle up higher for Rebecca to see. "Just now," she added with a slur. "Cold turkey. This right here was my last one."

Jenny held the bottle in her hands and studied the label for a few seconds before running her fingertips over it in a fond remembrance of what she was leaving behind. She then wrapped her right hand around the neck and swung the bottle backward so that it smashed against the brick wall that was behind her.

The sudden sound of breaking glass caused Rebecca to jump, and she reached for her holstered gun. Rebecca understood that, if Jenny wanted to, she could use the shattered end of the bottle as a weapon.

Rebecca stood from the couch. "Put the bottle down," she said with her hand still on her pistol.

Jenny dropped the bottle. It landed with a soft thud on the carpet.

"Please, sit back down, and let me finish telling you what I've got to say," Jenny told her.

Following instructions, Rebecca sat back down on the couch while easing her hand off the pistol. "Okay, go ahead," she said.

"After giving birth to Tyler, within the year the worst part of this disease kicked in. The rash didn't start until last year; it is one of the symptoms that can stay hidden like that for a long time. Even without it, the pain caused from the condition was unbearable. It was the joint trouble and muscle aches that were the worst. And as much as I regret it now, I went back to the alcohol. When it's bad enough, Lupus makes you have fevers and delirium.

"Sometimes, when I'm sleeping, I have dreams that seem so real. Right after Tyler died, I used to have a recurring one about the bag man, you know, that crazy, old cock-and-bull story that people around here tell to scare the kids? Well anyway, in the dream, Tyler is in the old, burlap sack that is on the man's back. He is kicking and fighting to get out. I have this huge butcher knife that I stab into the bag and cut it wide open, freeing my baby boy."

Jenny took a moment to wipe a tear from her cheek. "He should have been the inheritor to Abandoned Manor, you know?"

This part got Rebecca's attention. She realized with certainty that she had been right. Jenny had known about her ancestry and the inheritance. The only thing left for Rebecca to do was to determine the motive behind the assault on Rose.

Jenny continued. "But there was a stipulation in the trust that Mr. Blade had set up. Back in those days, it wasn't common for a woman to inherit a house and especially one that was as priceless as that. So Mr. Blade stated in his will that the property would be granted to the first male born into the family, but only after he turned eighteen. You see, it was going to be Tyler, but he died when he was seventeen."

It was the first time that Rebecca had heard about the age stipulation. "How long have you known about your family lineage and the details of the will?"

"Recently, I've been doing a lot of research into my family's past. And honestly, I didn't even know about the will or anything else that we're talking about until after Tyler died. I was surprised when I discovered it. I've learned along the way that everything is out there for you to find if you bother looking for it. What happened to Rose was my fault."

Rebecca felt her heart skip a beat. This is it, she realized—the long awaited confession.

"She was in her driveway yesterday because of me." Then Jenny shook her head and rolled her eyes. "I know what you're thinking, and no, I didn't do it. I'm not the one that hit her, but she was coming to see me.

"I had found out that the family of my great granddaddy, Ambrose Fletcher, used to run the greenhouses. I just wanted to see where he and Fay would go to see each other in secret. I was at the Bush's yesterday. I had gone to buy some new flowers for the front of my house."

Rebecca thought about the freshly tilled and mulched flower beds that she had seen outside.

Jenny continued. "I was telling Rose about how I had discovered my family's secret past, and she, in return, told me that her daughter had found a ghost story that someone had written about them. Then, the best part of the whole thing happened— Rose said that she also had the key to the old perennial greenhouse where the dramatic love affair of Ambrose and Fay had played out.

"After she closed up shop that day, Rose was going to take me out there to see it. It was her idea for us to make a night out of it. She was going to pick me up, and we were going to go to dinner after visiting the greenhouse. I was looking forward to it. It had been a long time since I had gone out with someone, and I could tell that Rose and I would become friends." Jenny stopped there, as if Rebecca knew the rest of the story.

And she did. Somebody, maybe not Jenny, had attacked Rose not long after the two women had been talking about the tale of Ambrose and Fay.

Rebecca replayed the events through her head once again, just as Jenny had told them.

"Was there anybody else at the Bush's greenhouses that day while you were in there buying flowers? Maybe somebody that would have overheard and had a problem with what the two of you were discussing?"

"William Vance was there," Jenny was quick to answer. "I talked to him while Rose ran inside to get the story and the key to show me."

Rebecca's heart began to hammer in her chest. She had been wrong from the beginning. It wasn't Jenny Braxton that had attempted to murder Rose Bush. Rebecca realized that she had been looking at the wrong ancestor of the Blades. It wasn't Fay and Ambrose's bloodline that she should have been focusing on. It had been Hayley's, who's youngest descendent, a male, was turning eighteen that night.

Rebecca rushed out of the house. Due to the steadily falling rain, water was gushing over the edge of the house. There was no gutter to catch the running water and force it to flow in another direction. She ran through the waterfall and to her car.

Why hadn't she pursued Pam, William, or Bartley Vance? It was because of Jenny's reputation, and Rebecca's own assumptions about Jenny's overall character that had pushed her mind in the wrong direction. She felt a stab of shame at this realization.

All she knew now was that, before she talked to anybody else, she needed to get a statement from the only other person that was at the Bush's greenhouse on the day that Jenny had talked to Rose—Mr. Vance.

As Rebecca drove by the Bush's property on the way to the Vance's, there was something that caught her eye. A white pickup truck was parked in front of the house. As far as Rebecca knew, there was no one staying at the old farmhouse. She knew that Tom was at the hospital with Rose, and Nandina was staying at the Vance's as requested by law enforcement.

She rationalized that the truck was probably someone that Tom had asked to stop by the house and check on the place from time to time during its vacancy. She also knew that being a good county deputy meant performing routine checks on people's property when they were not at home. And if she did happen to see anything out of the ordinary, she needed to examine the situation and make sure that everything was fine.

She turned her car off the road and drove down the dirt driveway that led to the farmhouse.

With the exception of one lamp that was shining in the window that was to the left of the front door, the house was dark.

Rebecca parked her squad car next to the white truck. After seeing that no one was sitting inside the cab, she searched the property for where the person or persons might be.

She reached to the center console of the car and picked up her flashlight. She pulled the poncho hood back over her head and stepped out of the car.

With the flashlight beam in front of her, she stepped around the truck and made her way up the creaky front steps of the house. She knocked on the door, but, just as she expected, there was no answer. Then she heard movement from around the side of the house. When she looked, she saw that there was a person that was moving quickly through the rain toward the porch. Even in the darkness and the rain, she could see that the person clutched a bouquet of cellophane wrapped flowers.

"Stop right there," Rebecca yelled out over the clatter of rain on the house's tin roof.

The person stopped and looked toward the porch where Rebecca was standing.

Rebecca reached her hand to her gun and moved closer to the edge of the railing so that she could get a better look at who she was talking to. It was difficult to discern any definitive features underneath the hood of the rain jacket that the person was wearing, but Rebecca could tell that it was a young man. Her immediate assumption was that the teenager was a friend of the Bush's daughter, Nandina.

"Is everything okay?" Rebecca asked. "I was just passing by and saw that a truck I didn't recognize was parked up here, so I stopped to check in. Do you need anything?"

"No, no, everything's fine," he said in a deep Southern drawl. "I'm not up to anything, I promise. My name is Jackson. Jackson Archer. I'm the boyfriend of the girl that lives here."

12.

BARTLEY GOT HOME from work around five-thirty in the afternoon and immediately went to the shower. When he came out of his room, he was wearing a nice collared shirt that was sky-blue, a pair of dark jeans, and a new cap. He knocked on the open door that led into the guest room and asked Nan and I if we wanted to go to dinner with him and his parents. Of course, we both declined.

For one, we weren't dressed for going out. I was wearing pajama pants and an old t-shirt that had a faded picture on the back of a large-mouthed bass that was jumping out of water. Nan had on a pair of white, cotton sleep shorts and a matching tank top.

And two, our minds had been working overtime with everything that was going on, yet, even with all of the mental hyperactivity over the past couple of days, somehow that night, our brains felt numb from the simple monotony of staring at the board game for the past few hours. The feeling was one of a nice cerebral respite.

"Well, I want to tell y'all before you find out from somebody else," Bartley said as he stepped further into the room. His voice dropped to a near whisper. "We were going to disclose this *huge* bit of information tonight at the party anyway, so it shouldn't matter that I'm telling you now." He stepped close to us and muttered, "I recently found out that I'm the inheritor to Abandoned Manor."

"Bartley," I said. "That's awesome." I didn't even know that he was related to the family that owned the place back in the 1920s.

"Yeah, I guess. Truthfully, the whole thing kind of scares the crap out of me." He laughed. "I mean, I don't know what to do with a place like that. Dad is looking into the best options for me. I didn't even know that I was *related* to those people, and now this." He lifted the cap from his head and ran his other hand through his hair. "It's a lot to take in," he said and looked toward the open bedroom door. "But don't mention it, okay? I don't know if Dad's ready for it to be out in the open just yet."

After Bartley left the room, Nan and I looked at each other. Between the two of us, there was an equal amount of astonishment.

I don't know *why* exactly, but I had a creeping feeling that something was off-kilter about the timing of the inheritance announcement as it stood in relation to when Rose had been attacked. To me, it just seemed like the pair of once-in-a-blue-moon type of events happening over the span of two days was *too* unusual, and for them *not* to be connected would be defying rhyme and reason.

However, I didn't mention this suspicion to Nan. Instead, we went back to the board game. I rolled the dice and moved my game piece up ten squares on the board. The instructions on the square that I landed on read that, until I was able to correctly answer a question from one of the cards, I was blocked from moving forward any further.

As Nan drew the top card from the deck in the center of the board, I started thinking. Was that it? Had Rose somehow been blocking the way to the inheritance? It surprised me that I was wandering down that particular train of thought. Truthfully, I *couldn't* imagine Bartley *or* Mr. Vance committing the crime. There was nothing that I could think of that would tell how Rose would have been a hindrance to either of them anyway. Had she *known* something?

When we knew that the Vances had left for dinner, Nan and I made our way downstairs to the kitchen. I poured us each a glass of the fresh-squeezed lemonade from a pitcher that I found in the refrigerator while Nan rummaged through the freezer in search of a pizza.

"You know what I love about these kinds of pizzas?" Nan asked me as she was unwrapping the plastic from around the pizza. "The little squares," she said. "The pepperoni and bell peppers are all square. When I was little, I used to love to eat them straight off the pizza while they were still frozen." She picked one of the pepperoni pieces off the top of the pizza and popped it in her mouth.

I laughed. "I've never heard of anybody doing that," I said. I liked the simple banter that she was giving. It helped to keep my mind off trying to rationalize a reason that Bartley or his father had committed the crime.

"Come here. Try one, and I promise you that, from now on, every time you cook one of these pizzas, you'll eat one of the square pepperoni before you put the pizza in the oven."

I walked over to her. Like she had done for herself, she pinched one of the little squares from the top of the pizza and placed it in my open, waiting mouth. She was right. It *was* delicious.

"Told you so," she said as she placed the frozen pizza on a round pan that she promptly slid into the preheated oven.

I found it funny that, even though the Vance's kitchen was equipped with a nice, brick oven for making homemade pizzas, Nan and I had opted instead for a frozen Supreme heated by the old, electric standby that was below the stovetop.

By then, it was raining heavily. From the French doors in the kitchen, the wet party decorations around the pool looked sad and unneeded. I thought that the scene looked abandoned with its unlit string lights that were running crisscrossed over the redbrick patio and the tables with their accompanying chairs upturned on the top of each of them.

Since Bartley and his parents had left, the power had flickered off a few times because of the storm, but it had come back on.

"Do you think that the inheritance announcement was why they made such a big deal about the party tonight?" I knew that what I was doing was leading to disclosing my suspicion. "I mean, I think it would be strange for a guy's parents to throw him an eighteenth birthday bash otherwise."

I was sitting on the countertop next to the oven, and Nan was leaning against the large island that was opposite me. She was eating a strawberry from a plastic bowl that she held in her hand. Before she was able to answer, there was the buzz from the gate monitor that was located in the corner of the kitchen. The sound startled both of us. Nan made her way over to it, leaned in close, and looked.

"It's Deputy Wooley," she said, sounding confused about the deputy arriving so late at night. "I didn't expect her to come back here tonight." Nan pressed the button that opened the gate.

A couple minutes later I opened the door, and Deputy Wooley was standing in front of me. There was a guy that I didn't recognize standing by her side. He appeared to be about my age.

From beside me, I heard a small intake of air from Nan.

Deputy Wooley was wearing a department issued black poncho, and the guy was wearing a nice, zip-up rain jacket over a white button down shirt and jeans. They both had the hoods pulled over their heads, and the rainwater was running down the water-proof material in little beaded rivulets. I noticed that the guy was holding a bouquet of flowers in his right hand. They were violet hyacinths; a flower of apology.

"Jackson, what are you doing here?" Nan asked.

She knew him. Was he a cousin or...

Speaking for Jackson, Wooley answered Nan's question, breaking my mental process of trying to link Nan to the stranger. "I brought him over here to make sure that you knew him. He was hanging out around your parents' place. He said that he knew *you*, but you can never be too sure, you know?"

"Yeah," Nan answered. "It's okay. I know him."

Out of the corner of my eye, I noticed that she looked at Jackson when she spoke.

"I wanted to surprise you, Nan," Jackson said as he held the bouquet of flowers out to her. "I brought you these. The lady at the flower shop said that these are the best flowers she had that would be symbolic of asking for forgiveness. They're drenched right now, but I think they'll be okay."

I wondered what he was doing at Nan's parents' house? Who *is* he, and, more importantly, how did he know Nan? What was their relationship? And why was he asking for forgiveness from her?

In the brief exchange that I had witnessed, there had been an easiness with them that seemed to be alive and well. I sensed a deep connection between the two of them. I could tell that they had a history together, but, what *kind* of history, I wasn't sure. I wanted to ask questions, but, at the same time, I was afraid of what I would find out.

13.

AND SO, I ran. It shames me to admit it, but that is what I did. When things started to get too complicated between me and Nan, instead of staying to hear things out, I ran.

SHORTLY AFTER ARRIVING at the Vance's house with Jackson at her side, Deputy Wooley informed Nan and me that we would no longer be staying there. Instead, she told us that another member of the Crow County police force would be staying with us at the Bush's place.

Nan and I gathered up our belongings, and then Wooley's partner, an officer named Carter Stevens, who appeared to be only ten years older than I was, drove us to the farmhouse.

Nan, Jackson, and I sat around the living room of the old house for what seemed like forever until it was decided among the members of the law enforcement that Jackson was not a person of interest. Promptly, Officer Stevens sent Jackson on his way back to Bishopville.

Afterwards, Nan and I went upstairs to her room. Even though we didn't talk much, we stayed up late into the night. The rain had slowed to a soft drizzle. The window was open and, in little gusts, the cool night air blew in, moving the curtains ever so slightly.

The knowledge of Officer Stevens being on guard downstairs gave both of us a feeling of safety. I still hadn't brought up my suspicions, but the fact that Wooley had moved us from the Vance's house only added to the disquieting scenario that my mind was spinning.

Nan was lying on the bed, and I was sitting on the hardwood floor with my back pressed against the wall. A lit candle that was on top of Nan's dresser made the room smell like lemons. I finally built up enough courage to ask Nan about Jackson.

"He's my ex boyfriend," she admitted with honesty.

The answer did not come as a surprise to me, but I felt a sinking feeling within my heart that his arrival would lure her back.

"Why did you break up?" I asked.

She propped herself up on her elbow and looked at me. "His dad was diagnosed with cancer and the doctors didn't give him long to live. Jackson moved away to North Carolina so that he could be with him. All of that happened back in the beginning of March. Dusty, listen, it has been a long time since I've seen or even talked to him. I have no idea why he showed up like that."

It sounded like she was defending herself, but against what? A question popped into my head. If Jackson *hadn't* moved away, would he and Nan still be together?

I didn't ask for any other details, instead, I said, "Nan, I wanted so hard to believe that two people can meet, fall in love, and live happily ever after." By then, I was getting to my feet.

"What do you mean you *wanted* to believe it?" There was the glimmer of tears in her eyes. "Things *can* be that way, Dusty. Being with you has restored my belief in that. I think, now more than ever, if fate intends for two people to be together, they will be. I just know that sometimes it takes a little bit of understanding to get there, and sometimes, there are a few complications along the way, but..."

I thought about the innate easiness that I had sensed between them; that irrefutable connection that seemed to be there. Cutting her off, I looked at her and asked, "Is *he* the complication or am I?"

Her silent hesitation told me all I needed to know—she wasn't sure of what her answer was going to be.

I left her alone and went downstairs to the living room where Officer Stevens was sitting in the corner with a shotgun laid across his lap. Nan didn't follow me. Instead, she stayed in her room. I eventually fell asleep on the couch listening to the night sounds on the other side of the old walls.

When I woke, it was a bright, sunny morning. With the exception of birds chirping outside, everything was quiet. It was peaceful. I looked around at my surroundings and saw that Officer Stevens was still sitting in the corner chair with his gun. The sight of him was jarring. It shattered the moment of bliss that I had felt, and everything else that was going on came rushing back to me—The Plant Killer, Rose, the inheritance, the recent idea that Bartley's father may have had something to do with the crime, and Nan.

I wondered if Officer Stevens had moved at all or if he had stayed in the same spot keeping watch over me.

I didn't see Nan anywhere and assumed that she was still upstairs in her bedroom.

With the officer's permission, I called Daddy and asked him to come pick me up.

It was on the way home that Daddy told me that Mr. Vance, Bartley's father, had become a person of interest in the attack on Rose. By then, the news of Bartley's inheritance had gotten out, with no help from me, mind you, and there was speculation among the police force that the delegation of the estate must have had something to do with the crime.

Daddy said that overnight it had become a known fact that Mr. Vance had been at the Bush's greenhouses not too long before the crime. Mr. Vance had overheard Rose talking about the inheritance with Jenny Braxton, of all people. Evidently, Daddy told me, Tyler was also a descendant to the Blades.

At the mention of this, I couldn't believe what I was hearing. It made sense to me then as to why the police had whisked us away from the Vance's house the night before.

I looked through the truck's window at the passing landscape. For the first time in weeks, the ground was saturated. The previous night's rainfall was one that we had desperately needed. Rainwater stood in the ditches that ran along the sides of the road. Through the tree branches, the sunlight glistened on all the wetness.

"Tyler was supposed to be the inheritor to the house and fortune," Daddy continued. There was a pause in what he was saying, but I knew what he was thinking—*Tyler was supposed to be the inheritor of Abandoned Manor, but Tyler died before it was passed on to him.*

It was then that I began to wonder for the very first time—had Tyler been *murdered*? The idea of it scared the crap out of me, but I didn't vocalize the thought.

"The only thing is," Daddy continued, "there is nobody that seems to be able to put all of the pieces together."

When we got home, other than the new deadbolts that Daddy had put on the doors, our house was no different from when I had left it two days earlier.

As usual, Gravel was excited to see me. He greeted me at the front door by stretching his paws up the length of my right leg as soon as I came in. I could never get enough of the contentment that he gave me.

Outside, in the back yard, the night-garden that I had planted in late spring looked replenished and healthy from the drenching rain of the night before. Even though it was late into September, the white peonies and angel's trumpet blooms were hanging on. The area where we lived had yet to get the season's first killing frost, but there was the undeniable understanding between us and nature that it would, without a doubt, be there soon.

I knew that the dusty miller plants in my garden would not succumb to the blow of that first frost, like most of the other plants would. I read somewhere that dusty miller is a very hardy plant, surviving even the harshest of conditions. In most areas, gardeners consider the plant to be an annual, but, where we live in the South, people around here sometimes treat it as a perennial. I thought about how some people use the plant as a placeholder over the fall and winter months until it is time for something better.

Had Nan, like Moira, used me the same way?

I went into my room so I could put my duffel bag of clothes away. The twig that I had broken off the nandina bush in Gran's backyard earlier in the spring was still on the top of my dresser next to the photo of Gran and Cranky at the summer bonfire. Over the summer, the leaves on the stem had become dry and brittle. The red berries were now a brownish colored husk of what they used to be.

Do you remember, way back toward the beginning of all of this, when I was describing nandina bushes, and I said that one of the characteristics of them is that the red berries are poisonous? Do you remember how I said that I would elaborate more on that a little later?

Well, here we are at later.

The berries *are* poisonous. I have heard that they contain a small amount of cyanide and that large enough quantities are deadly to birds and other small animals. Many gardeners recommend snipping the berries back from the stems and discarding them in the trash. This way, there is no danger of young, flittering wrens, kittens, or any other small creature consuming them.

Cyanide causes restlessness, headaches, nausea, and dizziness.

I was feeling all of those things that day.

I don't want to get too metaphorical on you at this late in the story, but I knew that falling in love with Nandina Bush had poisoned me. When I speculated the idea of Nan and Jackson being together, I literally felt sick.

Of course, it wasn't just what was going on with Nandina that was bothering me. The accusation of Mr. Vance attacking Rose, the revelation of Tyler being the one that should have inherited Abandoned Manor, and then the recent notion of my own that Tyler may have been murdered—it was all too much.

All of this was bad enough, but there was also the fact that the serial killer was still out there somewhere.

There was only one thing that I could think to do—I wanted to run.

I MOVED THROUGH the open air with a fierce intensity that I had not felt in a long time.

When I came to the end of the packed red dirt of Nesting Lane, I looked over my shoulder at Abandoned Manor as I passed by. I thought about the ghost of Fay Blade making her way from the house to where she would meet Ambrose in the old perennial greenhouse, night after night, proving that true love continued on, even after death.

I turned right onto the blacktop of Highway 378. Pretty soon, I was passing by old man Boston's small cottage. That morning, he was picking up fallen limbs that the previous night's storm had scattered about the yard. With a gloved hand, he waved at me as I went past.

I ran until I came to the familiar turn-around spot that was in the woods next to the Bush's property, roughly one and half miles from my house. My feet trampled across the dirt path as I made my way to the large tree stump.

As I moved down the footpath, my bare calves brushed against the weeds and the branches of the low-lying bushes that were still wet with rainwater.

I put my right foot up on the stump, stretching the muscles in my leg.

Through the thin line of trees, The Bush's property stood in mournful solitude.

I didn't see Officer Stevens' car, which led me to assume that Nan was no longer inside the house. I thought that maybe she was at the hospital. The idea that she had gone to Bishopville to stay with her uncle Colby even crossed my mind.

One end of the yellow crime scene tape that stretched around the property had come loose, and a long section of it flapped in the early evening breeze.

The sight of the two flags, an American flag and a South Carolina one, that were hanging from the front porch caused me to think about the previous day's news clip where they had been the focal point, driving the fact home that bad things could happen anywhere, even in a place as quaint as Crow County.

Because of the rainstorm, the ground where Rose had been found two days earlier was no longer the bone-dry landscape that I had imagined her body falling to and causing a cloud of dust to rise up around her. The rain had washed away any signs of a struggle that may have happened there.

The sun was disappearing behind the house where the darkening sky was aglow with a fiery color of orange. Soon the sky would be my favorite color.

In my imagination, I tried to place myself in the dirt parking lot during the time of the attack.

I pictured Rose coming out of the greenhouse. She was wearing a nice, black dress. The key to the old perennial house was in her right hand. Then, just a moment later, someone unseen hit her against the side of the head. Just as I couldn't see the attacker, I was not able to make out the object that hit Rose.

Rose was on the ground. Her arms and legs fluttered about in the dry dirt. With her black dress and hair, she resembled an injured crow. A cloud of dust was building. There was a figure standing behind her, but, as much as I tried, I realized that, without a clear motive in my mind, I could not put a face on the attacker.

These questions returned to me. *Why* would somebody have hit Rose?   Did Rose *know* something that the attacker was afraid she would tell? *Or* was the attacker afraid that Rose was about to *discover* a secret?

Going out on a limb with my wild assumption from earlier in the day, if Tyler Braxton *had been* murdered the year before, was someone afraid that Rose might discover the link between Tyler and the inheritance which would lead to the disclosure of the homicide?

Playing devil's advocate, I wondered who else besides Mr. Vance would have known about Tyler.

It all seemed to hinge on the ghost story of Fay and Ambrose. I thought about the old shoebox and zebra-printed notebook that Nan had found in her bedroom back in the beginning of the summer. I could not shake the feeling that the items that had been inside—a key, a ghost story, and several old photos—were pivotal pieces in solving the puzzle.

If Rose had been attacked because the contents of the box could lead back to the death of Tyler, who else would have known about the items?

Presumably, a teenage Kelly Maddox had shoved the box and folder underneath the radiator in her bedroom where they had remained for over two decades.

Then, something occurred to me.

Now, I want you to understand this—I do not want you to feel tricked or cheated, or think that I have not put enough red herrings within the pages before *this* that would rationally lead you, the reader, to come to this conclusion on your own merit. I'm just telling you things as I remember them and as they come to me.

A couple of years earlier, my ex girlfriend, Moira Everson, had mentioned to me that her mother had been friends with the girl that used to live in the farmhouse.

This simple, glaring fact meant that Moira's mother had been friends with Kelly Brighton Maddox, the girl that wrote the ghost story about Fay and Ambrose.

My phone was in the athletic band wrapped tight around my forearm. Sometimes I listened to music while I was running, but that day, because of everything else that was running through my mind, I hadn't even bothered to turn it on, and my earbuds had remained wadded up in the pocket of my running shorts.

I took my phone out and called Deputy Wooley. I told her my realization about Moira's mother. She said that she would look into it, and that was the extent of our conversation.

After disconnecting the call, with my phone held tight in my right hand, I began the second half of my run.

On my way home, soon after passing by Boston's house, there was a truck that was approaching. It didn't take long for me to recognize the truck as belonging to Bartley. He pulled up beside me. The passenger side window was down. I slowed to a jog and then stopped. I placed my hands on my hips. Because of running, my breathing was deep and satisfying.

When I looked at Bartley, I could tell that he was *not* handling things well. His eyes were bloodshot. Even though he was wearing a cap, the hair that stuck out from underneath it somehow looked disheveled. Something was wrong.

"You got a few minutes?" he asked me. "I could *really* use somebody to talk to right about now." His voice trembled when he talked. From the looks of him, it was obvious to me that he had hardly gotten any sleep the night before. He was worried about the accusations against his dad. I felt bad for him.

I walked closer to the open window. "What's up?" I was genuinely worried about his well-being. We had been friends our entire lives.

"Get in," he said.

I opened the door, and, after I was sitting down, I fastened my seatbelt.

He began driving.

"I guess you heard about Dad," he said.

"Yeah," I told him. "I don't think he did it." I spoke so quickly and bluntly that I hadn't even given myself time to consider if I should have said it or not.

"What do you say we go out to Pritchard's Pond?" he suggested. "Like we used to."

"Yeah," I said. "If that's what you want to do."

Soon we were turning down the dirt road that led to the old water hole.

Once there, he parked so that we were facing the water that was as still as a sheet of glass in the truck's burning headlights.

He rolled down his window and turned the ignition off. From the open window, I could tell that the night had become cool. I could hear the croaking of the countless number of frogs that had nestled down within the wet, grassy edges of the pond. I thought about all the nights that Bartley,

Tyler, and I had been out to the pond gigging for frogs.

Before he spoke, Bartley exhaled a deep breath that he seemed to have been holding inside for way too long.

Everything was winding down.

Bartley shook his head. "He didn't do it," he told me as he stared straight ahead at the water.

I didn't respond to the statement, but the silence that was between us was setting me on edge.

"Dad didn't attack Rose."

14.

REBECCA WOOLEY KNOCKED on the red-painted, solid oak door of the Everson family home. She had gotten to the house as quickly as she could after receiving the phone call from Dusty.

Now, the idea of Tyler Braxton's death from over a year earlier as being a homicide had added a new layer to everything. Rebecca knew that if it turned out to be true, there was a good chance that Mr. Vance would not be guilty of the murder.

Records from the attorney's office had shown that the Vances had not even known the details of the last will and testament of Thomas Blade until three months before Rose's attack. Therefore,

William Vance would not have known of Tyler Braxton's lineage.

From the curved, brick landing, Rebecca knocked on the door again. While she waited for an answer from the other side, she looked around the yard that stretched in front of the large, white house.

What she saw resembled the glossy cover of a Southern lit novel.

The early evening moonlight filtered through the thick, rubbery leaves of the magnolia trees. A vast garden of azaleas stood near the road, next to an ancient live oak that had an old rope swing hanging from one of its branches. The driveway was a plain, dirt path that hinted at a time long gone by. There was a yellow glow from the top of a wrought iron lamppost. Rebecca even saw lightning bugs moving around the tree branches and shrubbery.

From behind her, Janice Everson finally opened the door. Even in her late forties, Janice was just as prim and proper as she had ever been.

She was wearing a green and white chevron-printed blouse. She had pulled her sandy blonde hair back into a smooth ponytail.

Rebecca knew that Janice had been one of the popular girls all through middle and high school.

Like Moira, in Janice's hey-day, she had been the local beauty queen.

Rebecca cut right to the chase and asked her if she knew Kelly Maddox, even though she knew that she had.

"Kelly? Of course, we were very close during school. We've grown apart over the years, but, God, I hope she's okay." Janice placed the tips of her fingers to her chest. Now she looked concerned about the deputy's sudden presence at her home. "You're not here to tell me..."

"No." Rebecca shook her head, not letting Janice finish the question. "Kelly is fine. Do you know anything about a story that she wrote when y'all were teenagers? It would have been a story about the ghosts of Fay Blade and Ambrose Fletcher."

Janice laughed. "We were like fourteen at the time. That whole thing enchanted us. We even tried to start a little club. We were going to call ourselves the Azaleas of Abandoned Manor, AAM for short, but nobody came to the first meeting. It was just me and Kelly."

"I've read Kelly's story," Rebecca confided, hoping that the admission would throw Janice for a loop. "I talked to her yesterday, and she told me that someone she interviewed for the story told her that Fay may have had a baby before she was killed."

Janice nodded her head. "This might sound silly, but I wrote a little sequel of sorts about the Blade family's heir coming back to claim his fortune."

To Rebecca, what Janice was telling her didn't sound silly at all. In fact, it was exactly what she was looking for. "Who was the heir?"

"I don't know." Janice shrugged her shoulders. "It was just a fanciful little story that I made up. I've still got it if you want to see." Janice turned around and went into the house.

When she returned a few minutes later, Janice was holding a thin gift box. She lifted the top, flipped it over, and placed the other half inside of it.

Rebecca asked, "Did you know that Tyler Braxton was supposed to be the inheritor to the house?"

Janice paused and looked at Rebecca with confused worry spread across her face. "I thought Bartley was the inheritor. Moira told me..."

"He is," Rebecca said. "But only because Tyler is dead."

Janice swallowed a lump of anxiety. From the box, she handed a piece of notebook paper to Rebecca. "I don't know if this will help, but this is it. The sequel to Kelly's story. Like I said, it's just something that I made up. It's a fairy tale and nothing more. It's really just a couple of paragraphs. I don't even know if you can call it a story."

Rebecca took the paper from Janice. In girlish penmanship, Janice had written the story in purple ink.

Before she had a chance to start reading it, Rebecca saw that Janice was holding another piece of discolored construction paper. Her mouth hung open in shock at what she was seeing. She dropped the box to the floor where several other papers scattered out from the inside. Janice covered her mouth with her trembling left hand. The light from the moon sparkled against the enormous diamond of her engagement ring.

"Janice, what is it?" Rebecca slowly took the paper from her.

When she looked, what she saw was an inked sketch of Abandoned Manor. A boy and girl stood in front of the house. They had their hands clasped together. At the bottom of the page it read—MOIRA EVERSON AND BARTLEY VANCE 4EVER!

This is what it was all about, Rebecca thought, a girl that believed so much in a fairy tale that she would have done *anything* for it to come true.

15.

three hours earlier...Bishopville, SC

AFTER A BRIEF visit with her mother at the hospital, Nandina sped down the road toward the only place that she thought she would ever feel at home.

The late afternoon sunlight beat into the windshield with such intensity that she could feel the heat of it on her face and arms. It was as if she was driving straight into a gigantic ball of fire. Despite the sunglasses and the flipped down visor, the orange sun was nearly blinding as she moved toward it.

She knew that she had made a terrible mistake by allowing herself to fall in love with Dusty. It had been too soon after getting her heart broken by Jackson back in March. Then, the fact that Dusty had given up on their relationship so easily had hurt her more than she would have ever thought possible. It had been a misunderstanding on his part.

Over the summer, in just a short amount of time, Nandina had gone from hating the idea of moving away from everything that she had known and loved in Bishopville to unexpectedly falling into the cadence of her new home. She knew that a large part of her acceptance of the new chapter in her life had been because of Dusty.

Now, because of everything that had happened, Crow County had become a dark spot in her mind.

Even though the most recent weather that she had experienced there was heavy rain, when she thought of it, she imagined a dry and cracked landscape that was full of black crows.

As she drove down the highway, she felt as if there was no way that she would be able to get back to Bishopville fast enough. Through the open window of the car, she watched as the passing landscape gradually changed from red dirt and tall pine trees to the lush greenery of the boggy roadsides of where she had grown up.

Even though it was only going to be for one night, she felt like being back at home with her friends was exactly what she needed.

When she finally arrived, the swampy land was a solace. Even the deep, pungent smell of the mud soothed her, just as she had expected it would.

She parked her car right behind Mala's small, bright green truck and walked along the roadside, next to the dinged and scraped guardrail of the short bridge, until she turned to the left and made her way down the steep incline.

She trudged across the worn footpath to the spot where the old pickup truck sat.

Mala and Will were already there. They were sitting side by side on the truck's open tailgate. Will had his arm around Mala. On the ground, next to their swinging feet, was one of the five-gallon buckets that Will liked to use for collecting crawfish.

From the sky that was almost white, sunlight filtered down through the tree branches. Since Nandina had last been to the swamp several months earlier, someone had tossed several old tires onto the land where they had half-heartedly sunk into the muck.

Nandina took a seat next to Mala on the tailgate.

"You're going to need this." Mala immediately handed Nandina a spray can of bug repellent.

Nandina took the can from her, and, as she sprayed her arms, she noticed that there were already countless bugs hovering over her bare flesh.

"I see you haven't completely given up on Dusty." Mala took the spray can back from Nandina and placed it behind her on the flat bed of the truck.

Nandina looked at Mala with what she imagined was a face of pinched confusion.

"You're still wearing his necklace." With the tip of her finger, Mala touched the silver cross that was resting against Nandina's chest just below her collarbone.

Nandina reached to the back of her neck and unclasped the silver chain that Dusty had given her. She placed the necklace next to her within one of the divets of the tailgate.

A few minutes later, there was the unmistakable sound of an approaching diesel pickup. It was obvious that the truck stopped near the bridge, and then there was the opening and closing of a door.

Soon, a figure was making its way down the embankment. It was Jackson.

"Did you know he was coming?" Mala leaned over and whispered in Nandina's ear.

"No, but I had a feeling that he might."

In just a few short seconds, Jackson was standing in front of them. "I thought I might find y'all here." He was running his hand over the flat of his stomach. "So, here the four of us are once again, just like the old times."

If things had been different, the mere sight of Jackson would have caused Nandina to run to him and jump into his arms. In the alternate reality that she was imagining, she realized that if having Jackson was what she wanted, the happily-ever-after to their love story was there, waiting for her, just like the romantic tales that Mala liked to write.

But a renewed relationship with Jackson was not what she wanted. She knew that the harsh reality of things was much more complicated than that.

The awkward silence that hung between the four of them was unbearing, so Nandina finally broke the silence and asked Jackson if he would like to take a walk.

With Nandina in the lead, they made their way up the embankment, careful not to slip in the slick mud. When they got to the top, they walked along the edge of the asphalt.

"Dad's doing better. The doctor's are saying that he's going to be okay." Jackson was ripping at a large leaf that he had torn from a bush. "You would love it in North Carolina. The restaurant's garden is awesome. They grow whatever is in season. They have this chicken coop out back where they collect the eggs every morning. There's one chicken that they call Chickadee" He laughed aloud at the silly name. "Anyway, she follows you around and wants you to hold her. It's like she's a little dog or something."

Hearing him talk about all of this tugged at Nandina's heart. The truth was that all of it did sound like something that she would have loved, at one time in her life anyway. That is, if things hadn't taken several sharp turns.

She stopped walking and turned to look at him. Exasperated, she threw her arms out to each side. "Jackson, you can't just show up here out of the blue and act like nothing's happened. People don't drop in and out of somebody's life like this."

"Nandina, we can get back together. Where I'm living now is not that far from here. As soon as you graduate, you can move up there to be with me." He reached out to her in an effort to place her hands in his. But Nandina pulled away.

"It's over, Jackson." She crossed her arms tight against her abdomen. "Remember? It was your idea."

"So, what are you saying? You're in love with that other guy?"

Nandina shrugged her shoulders. "You said that you wanted us to see other people, so I did."

He nodded his head. "I see how it is." He turned his head to the right and spit on the ground. It was an action that she didn't think she had ever seen from him. "Well, I guess I should go then." He turned around and walked back toward his truck, leaving Nandina standing on the roadside alone with her thoughts.

FROM BEHIND, NANDINA watched Mala's truck as it made a sharp right turn onto the road that would lead to the Mujer's home.

Nandina turned left. She was heading toward her uncle Colby's place. It was where Mala and Will were going to meet up with her later.

Long, gnarled limbs of live oaks reached out over the asphalt making the road darker than it would have been otherwise. There was not another car in sight. This was a road of beautiful stillness and solitude.

Out of habit, Nandina reached her right hand to her throat. It was at that precise moment, when it was no longer there, that she realized that she had grown accustomed to the feel of grasping and twirling the silver cross that Dusty had given her. Her heart jumped at the realization that she had left Dusty's necklace on the truck's tailgate. Without a moment's hesitation, she knew that she had to go back and get it. Not only was the silver chain and cross special to her because it had come from Dusty, but the fact that it had belonged to his best friend must have made it irreplaceable to him. She knew that the guilt that she would feel if she lost it would be unfathomable. She had to return it to him.

She immediately flipped on the car's right blinker and pulled over to the roadside so that she could turn around. The tires roared over the textured asphalt as she pulled back onto the road heading back toward the swamp.

She thought about calling Mala and telling her what she was doing, but the spot where she had left the necklace was only a couple miles back. It would be quick. She would grab the necklace and be on her way in a matter of minutes.

After parking by the old guardrail for the second time that day, Nandina trudged down the embankment until she reached the truck. It was a relief for her to see that the necklace was right where she had left it. She hastily picked it up and was already making her way back toward the car when she heard the sound of something moving through the brush.

For a short moment, the old legend of the Lizard Man flashed through her mind.

She recalled how, in many of the accounts, people said that the creature had mauled their cars. Back when she was growing up, the photos that she had found in the newspapers and on the internet had shown vehicles that were covered in dents and scratches. Her young mind imagined sharp teeth and claws scraping against the metal.

She flirted with the idea that she would discover her car that way and nearly laughed out loud. Somehow, however brief, it had seemed plausible, but something about the sound tore her mind away from those freakish concepts. She knew that what she was hearing was the unmistakable squish and pull of rubber boots in thick mud.

There was somebody else out there with her. It was not the Lizard Man. In reality, and with the knowledge of the serial killer, the unexpected presence of a human was far more unnerving than the old monster story.

Nandina began to move faster toward the embankment.

Off to her left, the figure that she was hearing moved out of the darkness of the trees.

It was Moira.

"Moira, what are you doing here?" Nandina could hear her own labored breath. Seeing that it was Moira gave a certain level of relief to her thoughts, but there was also an inescapable creepiness about the other girl being there.

At the swamp, Moira seemed out of her element. She was wearing a green blouse that hung loosely over a tight pair of dark jeans. A long, silver chain hung around her neck. She had on a pair of rubber rain boots that were a close match to the color of her shirt. Her perfect blonde hair hung loose over her shoulders

Nandina looked to Moira's right hand that hung by her side and saw that she was holding what looked like half a set of garden pruners. Someone had taken the tool apart and all that Moira had to hold onto was a thin handle that the manufacturer had padded with red rubber. Sticking out the end of Moira's closed fist was the curved blade that reminded Nandina of the talon from a large bird of prey.

In an alarming action, Moira moved quickly toward Nandina.

Trying to get away from the other girl, Nandina was only able to take a couple long steps uphill before her right foot slipped on the slick mud of the embankment, and she fell flat on her face.

With her free hand, Moira was grabbing at Nandina's ankles.

While on her stomach, Nandina was kicking at Moira and clawing at the mushy ground in an effort to pull herself forward, but all she was able to grab onto were thin weeds that either slipped through her palms or pulled free from the dirt.

Nandina felt the metal plunge into her back. She screamed with agony.

Somehow, Nandina managed to flip herself over so that she was on her back. She tried to crawl away from Moira, dragging her butt across the ground, but the other girl continued the relentless attack. Moira fell forward and onto Nandina.

No matter how much she kicked and tried to scramble backward, or even to get to her feet, Nandina wasn't able to get an upper hand in the situation.

The blade came down for a second time. This time it plunged into Nandina's chest. She screamed again.

Her shirt was drenched with blood. The cotton was sticking to her skin.

Because of the amount of blood that she had lost, Nandina was weak. She wasn't able to move. The world was going dark. She was barely able to decipher the image of Moira standing.

Everything in Nandina's mind was coming and going. In one of the moments that she was able to understand what was happening, Moira was standing over her again. This time, instead of the sharp blade, she had a plastic shopping bag in her hand. From the bag, she was scattering green leaves and red berries from a nandina bush.

16.

"MOIRA KILLED TYLER."

The three words spoken from Bartley struck me with an unbelievable force.

I didn't respond to the simple, straightforward statement. Instead, the two of us sat in the cab of the truck in complete silence and staring straight ahead at the stillness of the pond.

By then, the surrounding sky was almost black and scattered with white stars. A nearly full moon reflected itself against the water.

"Remember when she gave us those cups that had our names on them?" he asked. "It was so she would know which one was his."

I did remember. To ensure that we didn't drink and drive, Bartley's parents let us drink at their house that New Year's Eve. Moira had been insistent on being the bartender. She poisoned Tyler.

After a long moment, Bartley finally turned his head toward me. "I thought Rose was about to figure out what Moira had done."

I still didn't look at him as he talked. I was too busy piecing together everything that he was telling me.

Over a year earlier, Moira Everson killed my best friend so that Bartley would be the inheritor to Abandoned Manor. I thought back to that particular time in my life and remembered that, when Tyler had died, I had been dating Moira.

"So you were seeing Moira behind my back," I stated bluntly. They had been together all along. Their "breakup" had been an illusion to divert any attention away from them. "You knew what she did. You were in on it the whole time."

I could feel my pulse quickening. When Mr. Vance overheard Rose and Jenny Braxton talking about the ghost story of Fay and Ambrose, it was undoubtedly the first time that he had heard that Jenny and Tyler were ancestors to the Blades. He must have told Bartley and...

Bartley was afraid that Rose would begin to piece everything together, so he did what he thought he had to do—he made sure that she wouldn't be able to.

He did it to protect Moira so that she wouldn't spend the rest of her life in prison for the murder of Tyler Braxton.

Out of the corner of my eye, I saw movement from Bartley. I turned my head to get a better view of what he was doing and saw that he was reaching into the front pocket of his hoodie. He pulled out a wadded, greasy red rag that he placed into his lap. It was obvious to me that something was wrapped up inside. When he unfolded it, there was one-half of a set of garden pruners.

My phone was in my trembling hand. I wanted to try to call for help, but I knew that as soon as I pressed the home button, the light from the screen would illuminate the cab, giving away my intentions.

With his right hand, Bartley reached toward me. He took the phone from me and tossed it onto the dashboard of the truck. The phone clattered against the plastic and slid across to where it landed in the far corner, next to the driver's side window.

"As soon as Nan found that old ghost story, we knew that y'all would eventually put two and two together," he said.

Based on what he had told me so far about what he had done to Rose under the exact same assumption, I did not like where he was going with what he was saying.

Very slowly, I eased my right hand down the side of my thigh so that Bartley wouldn't be able to see what I was doing. With just my fingers, I began to reach for the door handle. I could feel the hard plastic touching my fingertips.

I had to prep myself mentally for what I was about to do—pull the handle, push the door, jump out, and run.

I would do it on the count of three, I decided.

One.

Two.

Three!

I grabbed the handle and jerked it toward me while I flung the door open at the same time. I slid around on the seat and jumped out of the truck. Once my feet were on the ground, I nearly slipped in the slick mud, but I reached for the door and was able to steady myself.

I saw Bartley grab the red rag from his lap and toss it aside. The gardening blade was in his left hand. He flung open his own door, and, a second later, his feet hit the ground. He was moving around the front of the truck. It was the quickest route to get to me.

I spun around to make my way around the *back* of the truck, opposite Bartley, and slammed into somebody else.

Bumping into another person scared the shit out of me. I took a step back so that I could see who else was at the pond with us. It was Moira.

Bartley's girlfriend.

My ex.

Tyler's killer.

Like Bartley, she had one of the sharp blades in her hand. It was the other half of *his*, I assumed.

I bolted past her.

As fast as I could, I ran.

I ran faster than I ever had before.

I could hear Bartley and Moira running after me.

From behind me, I could hear their feet rushing through the tall grass and cattails that were growing around the pond.

The shining moon gave me enough light so that I could see where I was going.

I looked over my shoulder and saw that both Bartley and Moira were losing ground on me. This was one of the benefits of being a runner. I could haul ass when I needed to.

I made it all the way around the perimeter of the water and into the woods. I paused so that I could get my bearings on my location. Truthfully, I had no idea how to get to the nearest house from where I was without going back past the two maniacs that were after me.

There was the sound of human feet stepping on dry twigs and moving through fallen leaves. I knew I had to keep going or they would catch up with me, so I pressed on.

I had to push long, thorny vines out of the way and step over and around large, fallen limbs and even whole trees that had come down at some point in time.

Finally, I came to a clearing.

The Fletcher greenhouses stood in front of me. I hadn't realized until then that they were located within the woods that stood next to Pritchard's Pond.

My eyes darted around the area looking for a place to hide or something that would make a good weapon. The morning glory blossoms were all closed, but the vines themselves were as thick and abundant as ever. They grew up the sides of the greenhouses and across the tops.

I moved around to the back of the buildings.

The ground was cleaner back there. It was where Nandina had driven the tractor when she had dug the hole and placed the palmetto tree.

My mind was racing with what I should do.

I knew that where I was wasn't that far from the Bush's farmhouse, but I didn't think that there would be anybody inside the residence. If I *did* go there, and nobody was home, the doors would surely be locked.

If I were able to make it all the way to the main road, it would only be a mile and half to my house. *Half* of that to old man Boston's. But what if either Bartley or Moira had gone back to the pond for the truck?

If I were out on the road, they would surely find me before I made it to safety.

I went to the side of the greenhouse and moved my hand across the plastic to where it met with the cinderblock wall. I found a spot where the edge of the plastic had come loose.

With my right foot first, I slipped inside.

Even at night, the interior of the greenhouse was sticky hot. With the exception of the moonlight, it was dark.

I got onto my hands and knees so that I could crawl to a hiding spot.

As I moved across the dirt floor, I didn't think about the possibility of snakes or any other critters that may have been down there with me.

I made my way to the far corner, closest to the front door, where I hunkered down behind the old countertop. The blanket from the night that Nan and I had been together for the first time was still there.

Everything was eerily still and quiet. I knew that it was only a matter of time until Bartley and Moira found me.

17.

ECAUSE OF THE amount of blood that she had already lost, Nandina's thoughts and rationale were verging on the edge of delirium.

One of the last things that she could remember before she had slipped away into the world of the subconscious was Mala, Will, two male police officers, and three female EMTs that were standing over her.

Based on what Mala told the police, she had waited for over an hour at Colby's house for Nandina to arrive. After giving up, she and Will went looking for their friend.

"She's losing too much blood!" the medical tech said in an alarming tone of voice. "It's her lung. Her right lung's been punctured."

Nandina could feel her body being lifted and placed onto a board stretcher that the EMTs carried up the hill. The road was full of flashing blue and red lights. From the handheld board, they placed her onto a rolling stretcher that was moving across the ground within seconds. Lying on her back, Nandina could only look toward the sky; it was full of shining stars. They pushed the stretcher into the back of a waiting ambulance.

"She needs a tube," someone yelled.

They ripped her shirt open.

Promptly, someone was giving her a shot in the arm. "This is for the pain," the woman said.

Another person pulled Nandina's right arm up and over her head.

There was another woman's voice. "Because of the meds, this won't hurt, I promise."

Several inches below her armpit, Nandina felt the press of a scalpel against her skin.

She saw the woman with a long tube in her hands and, a second later, there was the odd sensation of the woman pushing the plastic tubing through the incision, past her ribs, and into the area surrounding her lung. The tube ran to a machine that would pull the air from around the organ so that the lung would be able to expand.

The pain medication caused Nandina to feel like she was floating.

Then, in the clearest vision that she had been able to experience since Moira Everson had stabbed her, she stood on a barren, cracked landscape that stretched endlessly in front of her. A murder of crows flew past. Some of them lit in the branches of a dead tree.

Nandina walked a few paces and saw that the ground that she stood on soon dropped off into a gulley. Below her, in the deep canyon, was a swampy land that seemed to be roiling.

There was movement to Nandina's left. When she looked, she saw that there was a woman that was twirling around amid several tall, healthy green topiaries. The woman's long, black hair hung midway down her back. She was wearing a yellow dress. When the woman rotated around far enough so that her face was visible, Nandina saw that it was her mother.

In this imagined world of the sub consciousness, Rose Bush spoke for the first time since being in a coma. "You know what you have to do." Rose pointed across the landscape.

A wooden framed doorway was in the gray sky. Through the open door, the sky that was on the other side was indigo blue. A palmetto tree and crescent moon stood centered within the rectangular passageway.

"You have to get back to the real world, Nandina. You know who is next on their list. It is up to you to save him." With that, her mother was gone.

Nandina reached her hand to her throat and felt the cross that Dusty had given her. She held it tight in the palm of her hand. Her goal was clear—make it through the door and save Dusty.

She took the first step down the steep hill.

She moved her way across the hard, packed earth until it became wet and soggy beneath her feet. The swamp had looked like it was stirring. The parched land had given way to a mush that was full of thousands of oversized crawfish. Some of the crustaceans were digging their way into the mud while others were crawling back to the surface.

Nandina's shoes sucked into the sludge as she began to make her way through.

There was movement in the brush. She caught a glimpse of a creature that was moving through the trees. It was the height of an adult man. Dark green scales covered its entire body. A long tail slipped through the mud and disappeared into the darkness of the trees.

A clawed, webbed hand reached around the splintered trunk of a rotted tree. The creature's reptilian head came around next. A long, forked tongue came out and slid back into its wide slit of a mouth. The eyes that peered at Nandina from around the width of the tree were burning a bright red.

Nandina ran. The bramble and briars tore at her skin. The further that she went, the deeper the mud became, making it increasingly difficult to move. With the mud slowing her down, she knew that there was no way that she would be able to make it to the dry land that was on the other side without the monster catching up to her.

It was then that she noticed that there was an abandoned truck that was the color of rust. Nandina made her way to it and was surprised to discover that the driver's side door was unlocked.

After she was safely inside, she frantically reached across the cab and locked the passenger side door.

On the other side of the truck's windshield, the sky was now dark.

She was half way to the door that was standing wait for her within the atmosphere.

"You get to be the hero of this story." The voice took Nandina by surprise. She spun around and saw that Mala was sitting beside her on the vinyl bench seat of the truck. The other girl gave Nandina a quick thumbs-up and then, in the blink of an eye, she was gone.

"Okay," Nandina was breathing heavily as she tried to collect herself. "I can do this."

All of a sudden, the whole truck shook on its axels, taking her by surprise. Something had hit it with all its force. Nandia screamed.

Outside the vehicle, there was a horrible scraping against the metal body.

Nandina spun around, and with her hand grasping onto the opposite vinyl headrest, she looked out through the back glass, but she wasn't able to see anything.

The scraping continued and quickly turned into a frantic clawing.

The pounding was at the passenger side now. In an inward explosion, the window shattered, sending tiny pieces of glass scattering across the inside of the cab and onto Nandina.

Nandina reached her hand to the door that was closest to her, and was just about to make a run for it when she saw something moving toward her. It was the same humanoid creature that she had seen slinking its way through the trees.

She realized that it didn't make any sense, because with him several yards away from where she sat, the attack on the truck continued.

So if it wasn't the Lizard Man that was doing it...

This time, when Nandina looked, she was able to see the truth. Moira Everson had been making the racket against the exterior of the truck.

Moira was wearing the tall, sparkling crown of a beauty queen. Her hair and makeup were done up as if she had just stepped off the stage of a pageant. She was wearing a purple dress.

Moira was reaching through the shattered window, trying to get to Nandina. Shards of glass were cutting into her arms. Blood ran down her pale flesh in tiny rivers that looked like veins.

Moira screamed. Something jerked her backward, pulled her through the window, and threw her onto the ground. The thick, black mud splattered up all around her. When the mud came down, drops of it fell on Moira's face and body like dark splotches of rain. Her purple pageant gown was filthy with the slop. As her arms were reaching out, trying to grasp at something, when a webbed foot stepped on her chest and pushed her deeper into the muck.

With his right foot, the Lizard Man pressed on Moira until she sank and disappeared into the depths of the swamp.

Nandina watched as the Lizard Man turned away from the burial and made his way back toward the truck. He walked around the front of the cab and reached his hand out to the driver's side door.

Nandina's heart was hammering in her chest as she watched the monster rip the door from the truck.

He reached his webbed, clawed hand into the cab. Nandina pushed herself away from his reach but quickly realized that he wasn't trying to hurt her like he had Moira. He was offering his hand to help her.

She placed her hand in his. The skin was scaly and cool.

He helped her out of the truck and lifted her body in his arms.

The Lizard Man carried Nandina through the thick mud of the swamp and all the way up the steep incline of dry land where he gently placed her flat on her feet.

Under the light of the moon, Nandina was able to get a better look at him.

While he was standing in front of her, Nandina thought that the creature must have been a good two feet taller than she was.

"Are you real?" She asked.

"Does it matter? Sometimes believing in something makes all the difference. Now, go."

She did as he said. When she was less than five yards away from the door, she turned around, wanting to get one more look at the unbelievable creature that had saved her. He was already disappearing into the knobby cypress trees that stood at the edge of the swamp. The last image that she had of him was of his tail as it disappeared into the dark, muddy water. It was breathtaking. Nandina felt tears forming in her eyes.

Then, breaking any sense of calm, a human hand caked with drying mud reached up from the edge of the cliff; the purple paint of the fingernails had become chipped. The sparkling crystals of the tall pageant crown came into view.

Zombie-like, Moira was clawing her way up from the depths. As she stood, it became evident that black mud smeared her face. Her blonde hair was dripping with stagnant water.

Nandina turned her back on Moira and ran through the door.

18.

one week later...

NANDINA'S CONDITION WAS rapidly improving. The doctors said that they fully expected that she would be back at home within the next few days. I held onto this piece of assurance as I made my way down the hospital's long hallway toward her room.

When I finally got there, the door was slightly ajar. From inside, I could hear the muffled sound of the TV.

I tapped on the door. My other hand held a vase of flowers.

From the other side, Nan called out for me to enter.

I went into the room and closed the door.

Nan was sitting up in the bed. She smiled when she saw me.

"Hey," I said. "I brought you these." I held the vase out so that she could see.

Deciding against a florist, I had put the arrangement together myself. It was made of several branches from a nandina bush, both the green leaves and the red berries, and an equal number of long stems of silvery white dusty miller.

At first, I had questioned my idea of bringing our namesake plants to the hospital. I thought that it might stir up too many thoughts about the recent murders.

I placed the vase on a narrow wooden shelf next to the window.

The autumn sunlight that came in through the glass was golden and added a certain amount of warmth to the otherwise cold and bleak setting. In the center of the room, the cross that hung around Nan's neck caught the light and shimmered.

"You just missed Colby," she said. "He went ahead to Mom's room."

"Are you ready to mosey on over there?" I asked. "I don't want us to be late." I looked at my watch as I spoke. We were going to Rose's room to watch the televised special where Rebecca Wooley was to receive a badge of honor.

I helped Nan from the bed. I knew that, even though she was still a little unstable on her feet, she had made tremendous progress. It was amazing that she was up and walking so soon after the attack.

"I can't wait for this to be gone," Nan said, talking about the tube that was poking out of the incision in her side. "It is so sore. It hurts every time I bump it."

I walked beside her with my hand on her arm to give her an added level of reassurance.

At the end of the hallway, we hung a right and walked through a pair of swinging doors.

We found ourselves inside of an enclosed bridge that connected the two main wings of the hospital. Both the walls and the ceiling of the passageway were made of glass. From the other side, the setting sun beat down on us. Colorful fall leaves blew all around.

By the time that we made it to Rose's room, Tom and Colby were there, and the press conference was just about to start.

"This is it," Colby said, and, with the remote, he turned the volume up on the TV.

On the screen, FBI agent Richard Tomlin and Deputy Rebecca Wooley sat in a pair of leather chairs. A female news reporter sat across from them.

Mr. Tomlin began to speak. "Last week, a months-long nightmare came to a shocking and dramatic end as two eighteen-year-olds, Bartley Vance and Moira Everson, were taken into custody by the Crow County police force.

"The bizarre case goes back to over a year and a half earlier when Moira Everson poisoned seventeen-year-old Tyler Braxton, whose imminent death would put Bartley Vance, Moira's boyfriend, as the sole proprietor to a family estate that is allegedly worth millions of dollars.

"Shortly after catching Bartley and Moira, Rebecca Wooley found an extensively detailed research by Moira that traced the Fletcher and Blade family lineage all the way to Tyler Braxton.

"The twisted agenda was supposed to be simple. The poisoning would give the illusion that heavy drinking and drug use by Tyler's own mother, Jennifer Braxton, during her pregnancy had caused a heart defect that ultimately resulted in his death.

"The already tarnished image of Jennifer Braxton was enough to convince the entire town that her actions *had* led to the boy's death, despite the fact that she claimed to have been sober throughout the duration of her pregnancy.

"A year later, the relationship between Bartley and Moira took a sharp turn when she announced that she would be leaving for college in the fall. The pair supposedly broke things off, but the breakup was just the beginning of the grand illusion.

"The couple stayed together in secret, and, over the summer, grew increasingly paranoid that someone would soon discover the sick truth—that Moira had murdered Tyler for the inheritance.

"The two people that Moira and Bartley were *most* concerned about figuring it out were Dusty Miller and Nandina Bush.

"Moira devised a plan that would assure that the two teens would remain quiet—she would kill them. She would make it look as if Dusty and Nandina's deaths were part of a serial killer's murderous rampage that was targeting people that shared names with plants.

"However, she knew that for it to appear as if a serial killer was responsible, there would need to be bodies.

"Over the course of five months, from May through September, Moira Everson murdered six innocent people—Mary Gold, Liana Vine, Dill Weed, Kimberly Fern, Pete Moss, and Scarlett Oak.

"Bartley claims to have had no idea as to what Moira was doing. As far as he knew, she was only guilty of one crime—that against Tyler Braxton. When he bludgeoned Rose Bush, it had been on impulse. He had been trying to protect Moira's secret.

"With the inconsistency in method of attack on Rose, the case immediately gained a lot of attention. People said that it was likely a copycat that attacked Rose, thus the search for the culprit was focused within Crow County. With so much attention close by, Moira knew that she would need to execute the rest of her plan quickly. It was then that she pulled Bartley completely in.

"In a statement to authorities, Bartley explained, 'Moira told me everything. She said that because of what I did to Rose, I was already involved, like it or not. At first, I didn't want to go along with *any* of it, but the more we talked about it, the more it seemed plausible that, in the end, everything would turn out to be okay. She told me that she was doing this for us.'

"Then, Moira attacked Nandina, leaving her for dead in the swampy land around Bishopville. But several hours after arriving at the hospital in critical condition, Nandina amazingly pulled through and alerted the local law enforcement to the identity of her attacker. She told them where they might find Moira and who she expected to be next on the list.

"Following Nandina's lead, Rebecca Wooley and her team apprehended Bartley and Moira in the woods behind the Bush's family home where they had Dusty cornered inside of a ramshackle greenhouse that originally belonged to the Fletcher family.

"So, it is with a great sense of pride that this honor is given to Deputy Rebecca Wooley of the Crow County police force."

Rebecca said that her medal was dedicated to me and Nan.

After the newscast, it was time for us to go. Nan walked over to her mother and kissed her lightly on the forehead. Mrs. Bush had still not come out of the coma, but we were all holding on to the hope that she would one day soon.

After saying goodbye to Tom, Rose, and Colby, I walked with Nan back toward her room.

For the past few days, I have been thinking about the morning glory vines growing over Fletcher's old perennial greenhouse and Mala telling us that the flowers symbolized true love's ability to return.

Since the night of the arrests, I have seen Jenny Braxton coming out of the woods behind the Bush's property several times. She told me that she had seen a whirlwind of leaves at the perennial greenhouse. She could have sworn that it was the dancing ghosts of Fay and Ambrose that were making the leaves move.

Due to the toxicology results on the exhumed remains of Tyler Braxton, it was determined that Moira's poisoning was not what killed Tyler, nor was it because of his mother's drinking. The heart defect had been hereditary, going at least as far back as Ambrose Fletcher.

Jenny and Ryan were working on putting their marriage back together. I no longer blamed her for Tyler's death. One of the biggest things that I learned that summer was that people are not completely right or wrong, good or bad; we are flawed.

Near the center of the glass-encased walkway, we stopped. By then the sky was dark. An array of glowing, white stars surrounded us.

"Dusty, I want to tell you something. After Moira stabbed me, because of the blood loss and pain medications, I imagined the craziest things. It was honestly like a living nightmare, but the scariest thing of all was the thought that I might lose you."

"Thank you," I said. "For saving my life. By the way, I'm sorry for running out on you like I did."

"Apology accepted." Nandina shrugged her shoulders.

I put my arms around her, accidentally bumping the chest tube in the process.

"Ouch," she said.

Hurting her scared me, but after realizing that everything was going to be okay, we both laughed and pulled each other closer.

the end

The Murders From Perennials

original short stories by Z.M. Strother, Liz
Wright, and Charles Campbell

BRYCEGIBSONWRITER.COM

Acknowledgements

There are a lot of people to thank for this one...

First, thank you to all of my family, friends, and anybody that has read my work and/or listened to me talk about it. This especially applies to my wife, Natalie, because I *know* I talk about this a lot. Thank you for listening. I love you.

Thanks to:

Pearl Fryar for giving me permission to use his topiary garden as the setting for one of the scenes in the book. Find out more about his garden at PearlFryar.com.

Laura Kirk from SC State Parks for answering my questions about crawfish and even going the extra mile of seeking the answer on a message board.

Deborah Rosier for editing.

CL Smith for the great cover design.

Those that posted my cover reveal on their blogs: Charity Rowell-Stansbury, Justin Bienvenue, and Leo McBride.

The authors that wrote the short stories that accompany the novel: Z.M. Strother, Liz Wright, and Charles Campbell. Their characters: Liana Vine, Dill Weed, and Kimberly Fern, respectively, are used in Perennials with permission.

All the authors that I have shared book signings with or met at various literary events: Charles Campbell, Rose Chandler Johnson, Victoria Hardy, Jerry Don Nicholes, Jae Johnson, and Gail Oust. I've enjoyed getting to know each of you.

Lynn Hazel and Jeanne Marie Peloquin for the character names: Scarlett Oak, Pete Moss, and Lily Lavellée. And everyone else that made name suggestions. However, in the end, I wasn't able to use many.

Jack Herzberg for giving Chickadee her name.

My early readers: Natalie Gibson, Norma Gibson, Dan Paxton, Charles Campbell, Liz Wright, and Hailey Wright.

And lastly, thank YOU!